If the RPG WORLD Had Social Media

STORY **Yusuke Nitta**

ART Character Design: LOL
Illustration: Yukinatsu Amekaze

DEMON LORD

PROFILE

mon Lord, ruler of the Demon Army.
I hate conflict.
y post on social media, but you are
welcome to contact me.
ask_demonlord@msr.mail.mmm.
e that I do not respond to prank
messages.

DEMON LORD
Um...

DEMON GENERAL 1
Ah?! What is it, Demon Lord?!

DEMON GENERAL 2
That looks like a really lonely "um"!

DEMON GENERAL 3
Is there anything we can do for you?!

DEMON LORD
Oh, sorry, uh...

DEMON GENERAL 1
There is nothing we wouldn't face for your sake!

DEMON GENERAL 2
Now...

DEMON LORD
Thank you, everyone

DEMON LORD
...Sorry, I'm heading out for a bit

DEMON LORD
There's someone I want to see

DEMON GENERAL 2
Huh? Demon Lord?!

If the RPG WORLD Had
Social Media

▶ GAME START

CONTINUE

BACK TO SLEEP

If the RPG WORLD Had ▶ Had
Social Media

STORY Yusuke Nitta **ART** Character Design: LOL
Illustration: Yukinatsu Amekaze

YEN
ON

NEW YORK

If the RPG WORLD Had Social Media

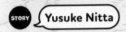 STORY Yusuke Nitta

TRANSLATION BY DANIEL LUKE HUTTON · COVER ART BY YUKINATSU AMEKAZE

This book is a work of fiction. Names, characters, places, and incidents are the product of the author's imagination or are used fictitiously. Any resemblance to actual events, locales, or persons, living or dead, is coincidental.

MOSHI ROLE PLAYING GAME NO SEKAI NI SNS GA ATTARA Vol. 1
©Yusuke Nitta, LOL, Yukinatsu Amekaze 2018
First published in Japan in 2018 by KADOKAWA CORPORATION, Tokyo.
English translation rights arranged with KADOKAWA CORPORATION, Tokyo through TUTTLE-MORI AGENCY, INC., Tokyo.

English translation © 2021 by Yen Press, LLC

Yen On
150 West 30th Street, 19th Floor
New York, NY 10001

Visit us at yenpress.com · facebook.com/yenpress · twitter.com/yenpress
yenpress.tumblr.com · instagram.com/yenpress

First Yen On Edition: August 2021

Yen On is an imprint of Yen Press, LLC.
The Yen On name and logo are trademarks of Yen Press, LLC.

The publisher is not responsible for websites (or their content) that are not owned by the publisher.

Library of Congress Cataloging-in-Publication Data
Names: Nitta, Yusuke, author. | Amekaze, Yukinatsu, illustrator. | Lol!, 1968– illustrator. |
    Hutton, Daniel Luke, translator.
Title: If the RPG World had social media... / Yusuke Nitta ; illustration by Yukinatsu Amekaze ;
    character design by LOL ; translation by Daniel Luke Hutton.
Other titles: Moshi role playing game no sekai ni SNS ga attara. English
Description: First Yen On edition. | New York : Yen On, 2021–
Identifiers: LCCN 2021021093 | ISBN 9781975323929 (v. 1 ; trade paperback)
Subjects: CYAC: Fantasy. | Fantasy games—Fiction. | Adventure and adventurers—Fiction.
Classification: LCC PZ7.1.K418 Am 2020 | DDC [Fic]—dc24
LC record available at https://lccn.loc.gov/2021021093

ISBNs: 978-1-9753-2392-9 (paperback)
       978-1-9753-2393-6 (ebook)

10 9 8 7 6 5 4 3 2 1

LSC-C

Printed in the United States of America

Once, there existed a position at the top of society known as the Demon Lord.

The Demon Lord's breath wilted vegetation. Earth decayed beneath their feet. Clouds darkened with contaminants when they soared through the sky. Every obstacle crumbled in the face of their unyielding charge. This creature ruled over all demons as the most powerful of their kind. They were evil incarnate, surpassing the gods with might beyond human understanding.

"Haaah…," sighed the Demon Lord as she gazed outside her castle, looking not unlike a young maiden thinking of a distant lover.

Once, there existed a position at the top of society known as the Hero.

The Hero was capable of breathing…but that was about it. His bones were wont to break from merely walking. Flying through the sky was a pipe dream to him. He couldn't manage to run for more than five seconds without needing to catch his breath. This creature was the weakest of all human beings, a shut-in with the moodiest of personalities who spent all his free time on the internet.

"Haaah...," sighed the Hero as he awoke in his bedroom. He was the kind of young man anyone could fall head over heels for... Actually, no, he wasn't—at all. Furthermore, what appeared to be a meaningful exhale was actually a simple yawn—the result of having stayed up way too late playing mobile games.

MOM

MOM Wake up 07:50

MOM Rise and shine 07:51

MOM My precious Hero 07:51

MOM Today is your 16th birthday 07:52

MOM The day I've spent raising you to be the most gallant child in the world has finally arrived 07:53

MOM Hero 07:55

MOM Hey 07:57

MOM I know you're awake 07:59

MOM I can see that you've read these 08:01

HERO Read 08:02 I'm still sleepy...

MOM Unbelievable 08:02

KING

KING How good of you to contact me! 09:15

KING Child of the brave Papatega Or should I say, Hero! 09:15

HERO Read 09:16 Hello

KING I would've liked to speak with you in person, but messaging will have to do! 09:16

KING I believe you are already aware of this, but the Demon Lord has been growing quite powerful. Something must be done! 09:17

KING My daughter, the Princess, has even been abducted! 09:17

KING So what I'm getting at here is...

I hope I can count on you to rescue her, Hero! 09:18

HERO Hmmmm Do you have a picture of the Princess? Read 09:18

KING Yes, here she is! 09:18

KING
09:19

HERO Father

I'll make your daughter happy Read 09:19

KING When did I say you could marry her?! 09:19

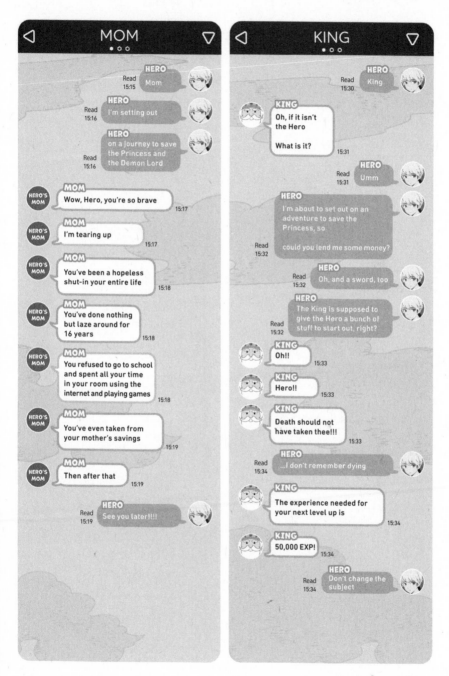

IF THE RPG WORLD HAD SOCIAL MEDIA...

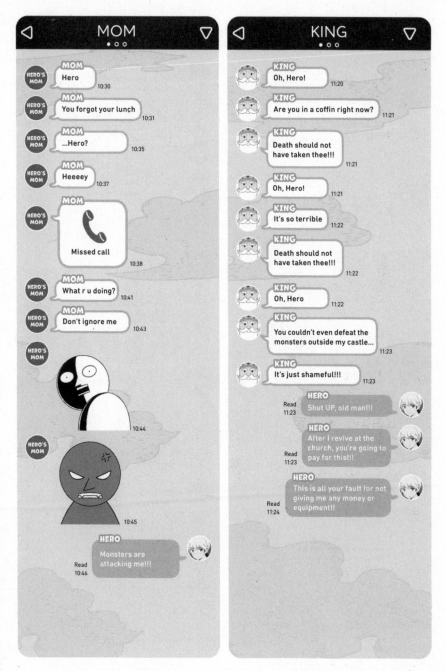

HERO
Hey, Demon Lord
Read 13:15

DEMON LORD
Hello, Hero
13:16

DEMON LORD
Get this. I finally beat the Princess at this racing game we're playing
13:16

DEMON LORD
You should've seen her face, hahaha!
13:16

HERO
...Sorry for interrupting your game

I have a small request
Read 13:17

DEMON LORD
Huh? What is it?
13:17

HERO
The monsters around my town are too strong
Read 13:17

HERO
Could you please tell them to take it easy on me?
Read 13:18

DEMON LORD
Hmm... Sorry, I can't do that
13:18

DEMON LORD
The creatures in that area aren't under my rule
13:18

DEMON LORD
Wait, hold on

I thought the monsters out there were the weakest and least intelligent in the world...
13:19

HERO
Stop it

I'm gonna cry
Read 13:19

DEMON LORD
Still, it would be unfortunate if you never made it here
13:22

HERO
Yeah, I agree
Read 13:22

DEMON LORD
So
13:22

DEMON LORD
I'll send a member of the Demon Generals from the Demon Army to be your companion
13:23

HERO
...Come again?
Read 13:23

DEMON LORD
She is the most powerful beastman monster in the world. I'm sure she'll be a big help to you
13:23

HERO
Nonono

That would mean allying myself with a demon
Read 13:23

HERO
And "beastman"? Sounds terrifying
Read 13:23

DEMON LORD
13:24

DEMON LORD
This is her
13:24

HERO
Send her over immediately
Read 13:24

DEMON LORD
Remember this, Hero
13:25

DEMON LORD
If you cheat on me, I'll curse you to death
13:25

HERO
G-got it
Read 13:25

Social media, also referred to as SNS, was first introduced to the world around thirty years ago.

One day, a sorcerer named Markie Goldberg, who had devoted himself to researching sorcery on behalf of humanity, hit upon a new way to use magic power after receiving a sudden bolt of inspiration. He invented a new kind of magical technology that took a shape similar to a spider's web. Then he accomplished something or other by merging that with this mana-type stuff in the atmosphere, and... Well, regardless of how he did it, the result surpassed even telepathy, allowing anyone in the world to easily send and receive information as long as they possessed a "PC" (personal computer), a "smartphone," or a similar item capable of transmitting magic power.

The following is an excerpt from Markie's overenthused statement about his discovery: "This is crazy! Am I really *this* much of a genius?! We can use this to connect with anyone in the world, no matter where they are. It works systematically like the threads of spider silk, so how about we call it the 'net'? I also feel like it's giving off *inter-* vibes, too, so why not *'internet'*?"

His subordinates heavily opposed the name because they didn't know where the *inter-* part came from, but because Markie was the world's first distributor of the service, the term *internet* ended up sticking.

As technology advanced, a great variety of convenient services that utilized this new network began to crop up. "Blogs" allowed people to share their own writings and journals publicly. "Facelook" enabled acquaintances to connect and share pictures of themselves. "Twittle" became a dumping ground for folks to post their idle complaints. "Instabam" gave those with a life an outlet to post pictures that showed how great they were. And "Rine" allowed people to send messages over the internet in either individual or group chat rooms.

Eventually, a revolutionary information company created a search engine that scoured the internet to instantly locate any piece of information you could want.

Twenty years then passed after the distribution of the internet throughout the world. The now-elderly Markie posted regularly on Twittle as he watched the use of his creation steadily grow, saying sadly, "I made that."

That was all he ever repeated in his old age. However, in his final hour, he delivered a speech on his deathbed that would still resonate with many for a long time.

"You know, I am happy that the internet has become so full of apps and services. Still, there's so much out there now that I don't even know what's what anymore."

His wife, who served as his lifelong partner and cared for him

in his final moments, responded with her usual headstrong attitude.
"Your point?"

"I want to unite it all under one term!"

"And what would that be?"

"Let me see…"

After much contemplation, Markie uttered a sentence that would echo throughout the annals of history.

"The internet is Super! Nay, Stupendous!" he declared.

"…" His spouse responded with silence.

"So it shall be called SNS."

"Any simpleton could have come up with that. But that is very like you," his wife replied with an affectionate smile.

Having achieved his lifelong dream of making his wife smile, Markie departed this world. He died a peaceful death.

And thus, all the convenient services on the internet were united under the term *SNS*.

His wife passed away several years later in the company of her sons and grandchildren. Even in Heaven, they continue their endearing married-couple comedy routine.

By the way, Markie and his wife will never appear in this story again, so feel free to forget about all this.

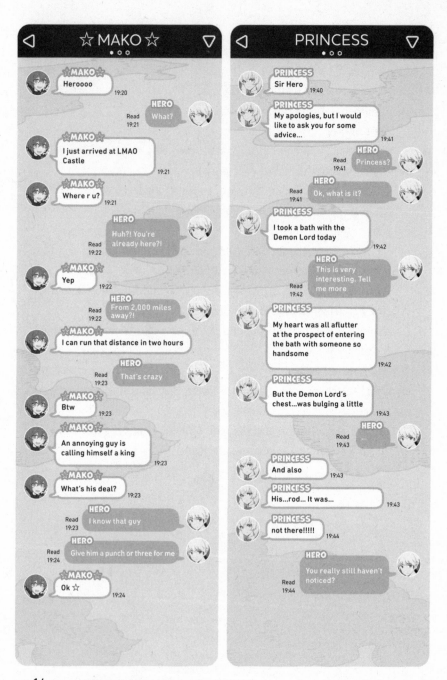

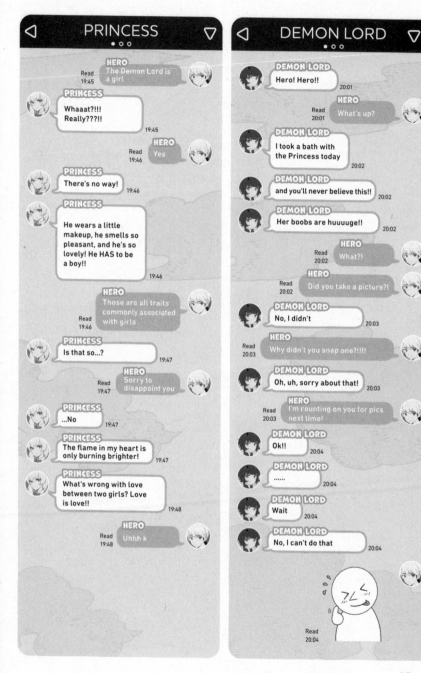

IF THE RPG WORLD HAD SOCIAL MEDIA...

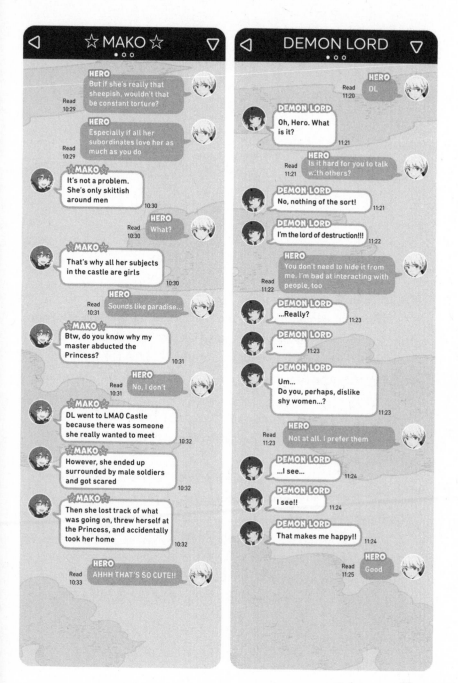

"Hmm? What are you looking at?"

Mako, a beastman monster and member of the Demon Army's Four Demon Generals, suddenly leaned her face close to the Hero's to get a look at what he was doing. Her upturned eyes and blank expression made her look adorable, and she even added a "meow" to the end of her question.

Since it was already past seven, the lighting in the forest was dim. That reduced visibility may have been the only thing that kept the Hero's heart from bursting.

"H-h-hey! Don't get so close!" he cried. The Hero was a shut-in who had severed all contact in his life, and he panicked and instinctively jumped back to retreat into the shade of a nearby tree.

"…That shyness is a serious problem, Hero. Not that I really mind."

The Hero was thankful for Mako's tolerance. It made him wonder (without any real basis) if all demons were as kind as her.

It had been one week since the pair had set out on their shared journey.

Mako had frizzy short red hair. Her adorable animal ears were covered in fur and protruded slightly from her unruly locks. She stood at around five feet, three inches and was somewhat shorter than the Hero.

Her black-striped sweater exposed her midriff. Her chest was of adequate size for an adult, and her top alluringly outlined its shape. As he was not used to interacting with women, the Hero had trouble keeping his eyes off that area.

Mako's long and well-proportioned legs extended from a pair of short shorts, though they quickly took on the shape of a feline's just above the knee. Every time the Hero saw her paws, he thought, *I'm not really into this kind of thing, but anyone with a furry fetish would be beside themselves with excitement.*

"It's getting dark, so let's make camp for the night. By my master's orders, I'm your traveling companion for now, so I'll make sure you're comfortable, meow," said Mako.

At first, the Hero thought that Mako was only doing the cat thing because the Demon Lord had forced her to, but she didn't seem to dislike it.

"What do you want for dinner? Ah, I guess there's not much point in asking. Roasted monster or animal meat is likely the best we can manage."

"…"

Without saying a word, the Hero took out his smartphone and began to tap the screen.

"Oh right, you won't talk to me unless it's over SNS… All right, message received! You're okay with anything. And there's no need to apologize. I'm having fun here," Mako replied aloud. Then she took off into the darkness of the forest to gather firewood and food.

She's awfully easygoing for a member of the Demon Army's Four

Demon Generals, thought the Hero, looking up at the sky. *She's friendly, though, so it's all right by me.*

Given how debilitatingly demure and inactive he was, the Hero never would've imagined he would leave the house for such a trek. He was even sleeping outside. That said, Mako was doing all the heavy lifting—making camp and preparing food every night. Seeing the girl make an effort to understand him and his communication difficulties brought a little joy to his heart.

Perhaps Mako was used to dealing with cases like his because the Demon Lord had similar hang-ups when it came to interacting with others. Despite having been on the road for days now, the journey had been nothing but comfortable. The Hero thought back to when Mako had mentioned that the Demon Lord's castle was populated entirely by women. He also recalled how lovely she smelled, and he briefly mused that the Demon Army must have it pretty good, all things considered. Before the Hero knew it, Mako had returned.

"I'm baaaack. I happened upon some lively-looking humans today, so I'm making human steak," she announced.

Mako was holding a large piece of meat, which she had already skinned and drained the blood from, over her right shoulder.

[No!!! You promised you wouldn't do that!!!] the Hero hurriedly typed out on his phone. [Dddddid you really kill someone?!]

After glancing down at her phone, Mako burst out laughing.

"Ah-ha-ha, sorry. I wouldn't do that. Even if I wanted to, my master has ordered me not to harm any humans. It was just a joke. This meat is from a wild boar I found in the plains."

All of the Hero's anger and fear washed away like air escaping a balloon, and he slid down into the tall grass around him...which he did primarily to hide that he'd wet himself a little.

"I guess from my perspective, that would be like eating the meat of a fellow beastman monster. I couldn't possibly do that... Just the thought gives me the shivers. I'm not nearly *that* twisted of a person. Anyway, I think I've got a handle on the sort of dishes you prefer, so I'll do my best to make you something delicious."

Mako then raised an index finger and, using what appeared to be a spell, summoned wood and rocks for a bonfire. Once everything was in place, she lit it with her breath, which was undoubtedly imbued with fire-element magic.

The Hero's birthplace, Beginnerland, had a warm climate and mainly consisted of sprawling grasslands. It got cold at night, however, so a heat source was welcome. The fire also kept monsters away, making it an essential part of the campsite.

"There we go," muttered Mako as she made the meat she was carrying on her right shoulder float in the air. She cut it into eight slices with an invisible wind-blade spell and pierced each portion with a stick. The cuts of flesh sizzled above the fire, looking very enticing.

The Hero's excitement grew as he watched the juicy fat roast, and his stomach growled impatiently as the aroma traveled through the meadow.

Mako had also somehow found the time to prepare him a flask of water and a perfectly sized stone chair. She left nothing to be desired, and for that, the Hero was grateful.

"Okay, let's eat. Oh wait, humans need their meat a little less rare, don't they?"

The meat had barely cooked at all, yet Mako took one stick with both hands and heartily sank her teeth into a slice. Such an action seemed appropriate for a beastman monster, and the sight proved amusing to the Hero.

"Hmm?"

As the Hero reached out from the opposite side of the fire to grab some meat, Mako felt a vibration in her back pocket.

"…Which group did I set to vibrate again?" she asked, pulling out a cute phone colored an unusual shade of pink and checking her messages.

This prompted a question in the Hero's mind.

[Oh yeah, you said you're a member of the Demon Army's Four Demon Generals, right? What are the other three members like?] he asked using his phone.

Mako was looking at her group chat when she noticed the Hero's message.

"Hmm…," she began, screwing up her face in a way that was rare for her. "It's difficult to explain."

"…" The Hero responded with silence.

"They're all pretty weird, I guess."

"Huh…," the Hero said aloud unconsciously, with only the bright-red fire to illuminate his surprised expression in the night.

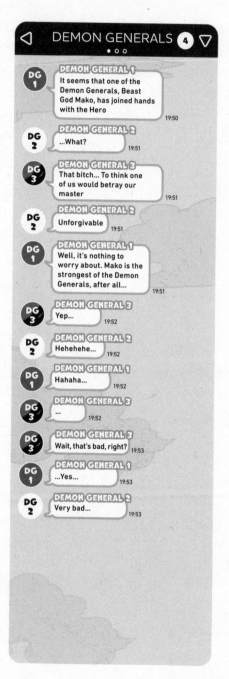

☆MAKO☆
What are you all talking about?
Read 19:54

DEMON GENERAL 1
Mako! You bitch!!
19:55

DEMON GENERAL 2
Traitor! Pervert! Hottie!
19:55

DEMON GENERAL 3
Screw you and your adorable catlike features!
19:55

☆MAKO☆
What? Uh, thanks lol
Read 19:56

DEMON GENERAL 1
So, Mako...
why did you betray our master?
19:56

☆MAKO☆
Huh? I don't recall doing that
Read 19:56

DEMON GENERAL 2
Huh?
19:56

DEMON GENERAL 3
You joined the Hero, right?
19:57

☆MAKO☆
Oh, that. Master ordered me to
Read 19:57

DEMON GENERAL 2
?????
19:57

DEMON GENERAL 1
(What is going on...?)
19:58

☆MAKO☆
And so on and so forth
Read 20:15

☆MAKO☆
That's what happened ☆
Read 20:16

DEMON GENERAL 1
I still don't get it
20:16

DEMON GENERAL 2
Why would the Demon Lord assist the Hero...?
20:16

☆MAKO☆
Maybe
Read 20:16

☆MAKO☆
because it's boring if her enemy is weak? Idk
Read 20:17

☆MAKO☆
Anyway, why are you all using those names and weird icons?

This is difficult to follow
Read 20:17

DEMON GENERAL 3
It's not difficult at all!!
20:18

DEMON GENERAL 1
It's vital that the Demon Generals project an imposing aura!!
20:18

DEMON GENERAL 2
It's important!!
20:19

DEMON GENERAL 1
I'm also shy about showing my face online!
20:19

DEMON GENERAL 2
I'm shy, too!!!
20:19

☆MAKO☆
You guys are always so difficult
Read 20:19

Meanwhile, the Demon Lord and the Hero were happily messaging each other. They exchanged texts every day—mostly about trivial things.

They asked the other's ages, if they had any hobbies, about their favorite foods, what they did in their free time, how much television they watched, and whether they liked pineapple on pizza. None of these were questions that especially needed to be posited. Yet both sides continued to toss inquiries as though afraid that the conversation would come to a permanent end if they stopped.

Neither had seen the other in person, but the pair had developed a friendship thanks to the internet. Their profile pictures provided a glimpse at their partner's appearance, and the messages gave each of them a good grasp of their counterpart's personality, even if they only had words to go off.

One thing they had in common was how comfortable, even relaxed, they both felt about exchanging messages over SNS. It was as if they were lovers in a previous life separated by social position, trying to regain lost time from a tragic past in which they were denied the chance to meet. They were texting at every possible opportunity.

[Btw, where are you now, Hero?]

[Hmm?]

[Well… You told me that you left on your journey, but I've been wondering how far you've traveled.]

[Oh, uh… Let me think. Right now, I'm in Beginnerland. I started from LMAO Castle Town, which is where I live.]

[Okay.]

[This is day ten of my journey, and I feel like we're finally approaching the next town.]

When she saw that, the Demon Lord quickly closed the chat on her smartphone, searched *town near LMAO Castle Town*, and found a map.

[Oh, does that mean you're approaching Lafta?]

Just like the Demon Lord had, the Hero closed the text app and searched the name of that settlement.

[Yeah, it looks like it. You have an impressive knowledge of the region, DL.]

[Like I said, I want to help you.]

[I appreciate that, but…]

The Hero was about to point out that he and the Demon Lord were supposed to be enemies… However, he quickly decided that was a pointless exercise and could be taken as insensitive.

[…Wait, Lafta is only about twelve miles from LMAO Castle. If it's taken you ten days to get this far, then you must be taking it pretty easy, huh?]

The Hero's heart skipped a beat at the Demon Lord's sudden probing inquiry.

[No, no! That's not it. I just tend to move slowly when I travel. Ha-ha-ha...]

I'm not really going slow because I want to, though..., thought the Hero. He then nonchalantly changed the subject.

[Anyway, I'm excited to sleep in a bed for the first time in ten days.]

[...I see. So has resting outside been hard for you?]

[It was tough at first because of the hard ground and the bugs, but I've been steadily getting used to it. Mako's presence has kept monsters away, which is a huge help. Sleeping outside has felt like camping, so it's been fun...I guess. I've never roughed it before, though.]

[...Remember, Hero...]

[Hmm?]

[If you cheat on me with Mako...]

[I'm telling you, I'm not going to do that, lol. I've never even had a girlfriend...]

The Demon Lord's face instantly lit up. She had assumed the Hero didn't have a girlfriend because of the way he'd said [*Marry me, you goddamn bitch!!!!!]* the first day they had exchanged messages, but him admitting as much was still a relief.

She was aware that there were men in the world who tricked women with similar lies. Still, she had been messaging him for over ten days, and he always responded instantly, so the Demon Lord thought it unlikely that he was taken.

[...Since we're on the topic, do you have a boyfriend, DL?] the Hero nervously questioned.

He could only judge the Demon Lord's appearance from her profile icon, but she looked beautiful and cool. Given her title, she undoubtedly resided in an enormous castle. It was impossible to imagine she wasn't popular with guys. However...

[No!!! Of course I don't! I've never had one!]

Even through text, her panic was palpable.

The Hero was relieved. Mako had told him that the Demon Lord was extremely shy, just like him. What's more, her messages had all given off innocent vibes. Her frenetic replies allowed the Hero to accept that she most likely didn't have a boyfriend.

That night, the Hero and Mako safely reached the town of Lafta. Thinking it would be problematic if a member of the Demon Army's Four Demon Generals just strolled into a human settlement, the Hero insisted that Mako sleep outside as per usual while he looked for an inn.

"Oh, don't worry about it. I usually rest in the open air at the Demon Lord's castle anyway. I find it easier to relax in the trees than on a bed," Mako responded with her usual easygoing nature after the Hero apologized to her.

In reply, the Hero responded with a quick message saying [thx!]

Although he had stated he would be spending the night at an inn, a room in such places had become quite expensive lately. Thus, he elected to search for a twenty-four-hour business called an "internet café." Lodging was much cheaper there.

Usually, adventurers made a living selling valuable items that monsters occasionally dropped, such as fangs and pelts. However, as Mako had been serving as his bodyguard for the entirety of this journey, the Hero hadn't battled anything. All he had on him was a little bit of money from his mom.

The young man had caused his mother no end of trouble by spending way too much money on the *gacha* games on his phone while shut away in his room. He felt guilty about his wasteful spending habits.

I've never saved money before, and Mom was so relieved that I finally left home. I can't ask her for more cash... I'll have to do my best to save from now on, the Hero decided.

Perhaps because of some painful experience in his past, walking through Lafta alone made him feel somewhat on edge. However, as he had spent his whole existence as a shut-in, he was happy to be able to sleep inside again, and he was looking forward to showering.

"Hmm? Are you staying at an internet café?"

As the Hero was searching for a place to stay on his smartphone, Mako's face suddenly filled his field of vision.

"...!"

Flustered, the Hero leaped backward and sent her a message.

[I told you not to get so close! You scared me!]

"I can't help it," Mako pouted, turning her back to him. "Anyway, why aren't you staying at an inn? I'm pretty sure you'd get a better rest there. Don't you have to sleep in a chair at internet cafés?"

[...]

"What's that silent message supposed to mean?"

The Hero sulked. Naturally, he would have liked a relaxing night in a proper bed, but he wasn't about to admit he couldn't afford it.

"Ah, do you not have any money, Hero?"

Mako's words pierced the young man's fragile pride as surely as any arrow.

[...No, nothing like that! I have money!]

"Then you should just stay at an inn."

[I just really love the internet, ha-ha-ha...]

At this point, it was about nothing more than keeping Mako from discovering how poor he was.

"You know modern inns are fully equipped with computers and internet, right?"

Mako performed a quick search on her smartphone. Lafta inns charged five thousand GP for one night, while internet cafés charged two thousand GP. The problem was, the Hero only had three thousand GP in his wallet.

"..."

Silence fell as the Hero broke into a cold sweat. Mako then glanced at the Hero and unintentionally poured salt in the wound.

"Wait, don't most adventurers get the money they need by exterminating monsters?"

She hadn't meant any harm, but her words painfully tugged at the guilt the Hero harbored over his lazy lifestyle. Unfortunately, now that he had committed to preventing her from learning of his financial woes, he couldn't back down.

"...You know, I've been wondering about something."

Mako's next question, however, got to the real heart of the issue.

"...Hero, are you weak?"

And there was the real reason he couldn't afford an inn.

The Hero had been trying to conceal this, but he'd never seen a real battle in his life. His mom had told him that he was an energetic child who loved to play outside, but he suddenly became a recluse one day. As far as the Hero knew, he had never defeated a monster and gained experience points, and his level had never risen.

All this indoor time had worn away at his physical reflexes, too. It typically took people two days to travel from LMAO Castle Town to Lafta, but the Hero had needed ten. That was partially due to him telling Mako that they should enjoy the trip, but that was a cover-up. Ten minutes of walking was enough to leave him panting from exhaustion.

[No, I'm not weak!]

Backed into a corner, the Hero made an obvious bluff. It may have started as simply wanting to keep up appearances, but now his male bravado was kicking in—he didn't want to look uncool in front of a girl.

He had already told the Demon Lord that he was unable to defeat the monsters. It had come up in the flow of conversation, and the Hero hadn't felt the need to hide it then. Curiously, admitting as much to her had felt okay. It may have been that being honest was easier via text than when face-to-face with someone.

"Okay. Then starting tomorrow, can I leave the fighting to you?" Mako requested cheerfully, bobbing her animal ears up and down. She looked as if she couldn't wait to witness the Hero's strength.

[…I don't know about that…] he reluctantly replied after a little hesitation.

"…You really *are* weak, aren't you?"

[No, I'm not!!!]

"Are you sure? It sounds like you're lying. Can you actually fight?"

Mako seemed genuinely curious, but the Hero was at the end of his rope, finding it more and more challenging to keep up the facade with every passing moment. Finally, he couldn't take it anymore and screamed, "*What did you say?! I'll show you how the Hero fights! Just you wait!!!*"

It was a desperate move to protect his pride and the unfortunate result of a string of fibs.

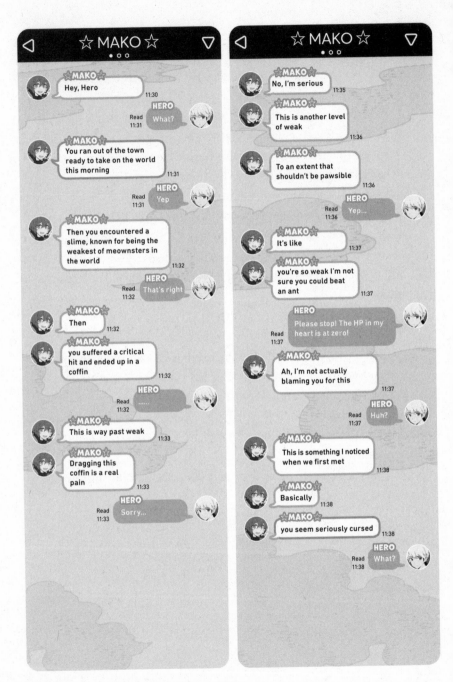

PRIEST

PRIEST: O Hero! 12:50

PRIEST: You have been cursed! 12:51

HERO: I know that already (Read 12:51)

HERO: Do you know what kind it is? (Read 12:51)

PRIEST: You are actually suffering from 108 different ones! 12:51

HERO: That's a lot!! (Read 12:52)

HERO: Well, whatever. Lift them please (Read 12:52)

PRIEST: Oogly Boogly Woogly! ♪ 12:52

PRIEST: Bad news. These curses are imbued with enough magic power to fill a galaxy 12:52

PRIEST: There is nothing I can do about them! 12:53

HERO: Huh... (Read 12:53)

PRIEST: O poor Hero! I shall pray for you! 12:53

PRIEST: Amen. Ramen. 12:54

PRIEST: I'm so handsem!! 12:54

HERO: I'll kill you (Read 12:54)

DEMON LORD

DEMON LORD: Hero! Hero! 18:50

DEMON LORD: I played a VVR racing game with the Princess today 18:51

DEMON LORD: You should've seen her, haha

She got so into it that her whole body was hunched over toward the TV. It was so cute 18:51

HERO: Cool... (Read 18:51)

DEMON LORD: Hmm? 18:52

DEMON LORD: What is it, Hero?

Are you feeling okay? 18:52

HERO: Nah, I'm fine (Read 18:52)

DEMON LORD: Really? 18:53

DEMON LORD: No, something must have happened. You're not yourself 18:53

HERO: ... (Read 18:53)

DEMON LORD: Um...
You can talk to me 18:53

DEMON LORD: I'll listen... 18:53

HERO: Thanks, DL (Read 18:54)

YUSUKE NITTA 35

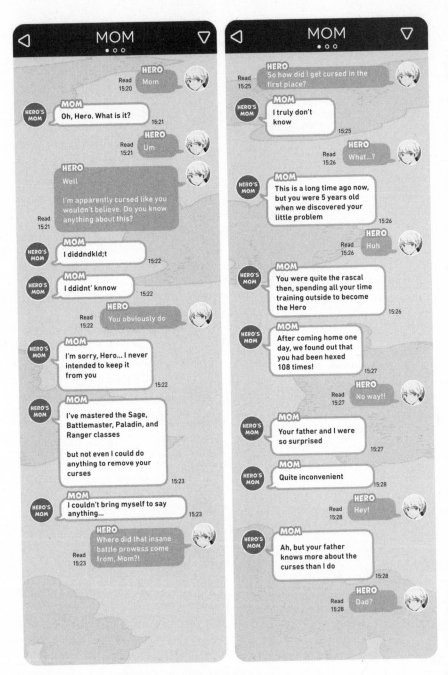

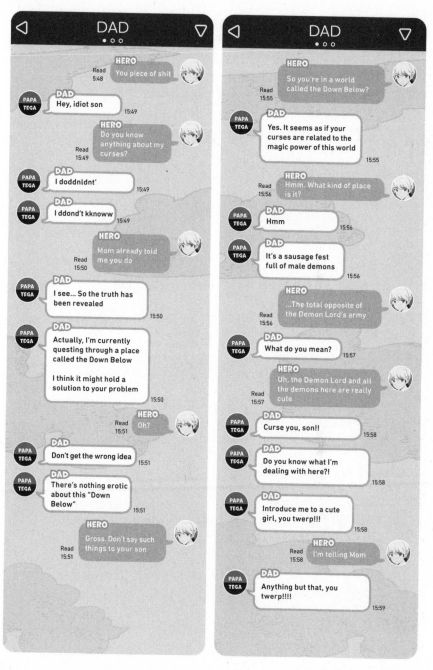

IF THE RPG WORLD HAD SOCIAL MEDIA...

☆ MAKO ☆

HERO
Why the heck was that bizarre world created?
Read 18:16

☆MAKO☆
Well
18:16

☆MAKO☆
you know how the Demon Lord is shy with men?
18:16

HERO
Yeah
Read 18:17

☆MAKO☆
One day, she drove all the male demons, including the Demon Overlord, away and forced them into the Down Below
18:17

HERO
Talk about thorough...
Read 18:17

☆MAKO☆
There were reasons besides her nervousness
18:17

HERO
I'm surprised the Demon Overlord and all the male demons just went along with it That's no small task, asking them to leave their homes
Read 18:17

☆MAKO☆
No one can oppose her
18:17

☆MAKO☆
The Demon Lord has a natural ability only seen in a demon once every 500,000,000 years
18:17

HERO
Whoa
Read 18:18

☆MAKO☆
Simply put, she's 16 times stronger than her dad
18:18

HERO
Whoa
Read 18:18

DEMON LORD

HERO
DL
Read 18:45

DEMON LORD
...She told you, huh?
18:46

HERO
Uh... Yeah. Sorry
Read 18:46

HERO
I heard about how you banished your dad and all the male demons
Read 18:46

DEMON LORD
Aaaaaa...
18:46

HERO
There's no reason to feel so bad about it lol
Read 18:46

HERO
Mako told me there was a good motive for it. She said a lot of female demons were being sexually harassed
Read 18:46

DEMON LORD
I guess...
18:47

DEMON LORD
But I still used my power to chase them all away
18:47

DEMON LORD
Don't you think that makes me crazy and selfish?
18:47

HERO
Not really. I think you're a wonderful girl who's considerate of others
Read 18:47

DEMON LORD
Hero
18:48

HERO
Hmm?
Read 18:48

DEMON LORD
I'm happy...
18:49

DEMON LORD
That's the first time anyone's called me a girl...
18:49

HERO
Ahhh, you're so cute!!
Read 18:50

YUSUKE NITTA   39

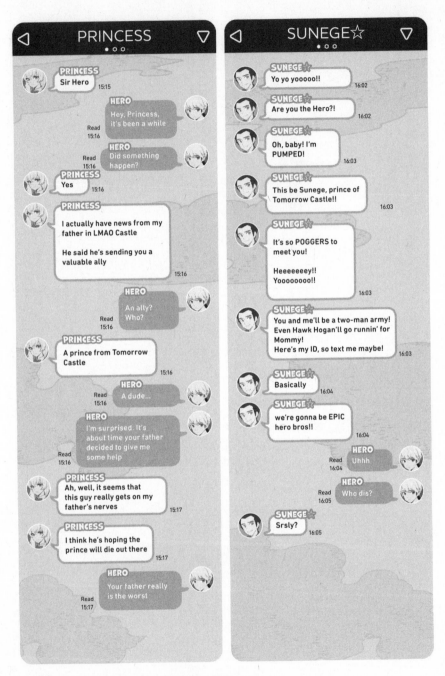

"All right, I'll be back in a meowment!" Mako chirped. After stowing her smartphone in a back pocket of her pants, she raced off with a high-pitched *boom*.

Mako moved way too fast for the eyes of the cursed Hero to follow, but he was able to understand that she was headed toward Tomorrow Castle to find the prince.

Doubt entered the Hero's mind as he stood there. *Was telling her to kick his ass going too far? Did he really do anything to make me that angry?* That line of thought lasted for about five seconds before he decided, *Eh, it's fine. He was annoying.*

He didn't consider it for very long. Death didn't mean much in this world because churches revived those who had fallen. Tomorrow Castle undoubtedly had priests. Sunege would be just fine.

...I can't believe he called the Demon Lord a pest. She's a good person.

Thinking of the Demon Lord helped the Hero calm down. He recalled what she'd mentioned about Mako's battle prowess. If he remembered correctly, the Demon Lord had said she was the fastest in the Demon Army, had four-hit attacks, possessed elite spells, and was capable of destroying a town in no time at all.

"…I might as well send Mako a message asking her not to kill him."

Unbidden sympathy for Sunege welled up in the Hero. He texted Mako, then put his smartphone in his bag and stretched, as if a weight had been lifted off his shoulders.

"…Wait. This place is…," the Hero began, but he'd noticed too late. He was currently in a famous wetland rumored to be inhabited by the strongest monsters in Beginnerland. Wandering it alone was a bad idea for someone with no combat ability.

"Grrrr…"

As would be expected, the creatures of the fen did not take kindly to someone invading their territory. They had been keeping their distance because of Mako's presence, but now she was gone, and the Hero suddenly found himself faced with a kobold. The monster let fly a dog-like howl, and more of its kin appeared.

"W-wait, stop! I can't fight! Time-out, time-out!!!"

Perhaps this was karma. The Hero mustered more effort than he had in his entire life—fleeing.

Mako had reached the outskirts of Tomorrow Castle Town. There were two gatekeepers watching for trespassers by the town gate, so she decided to observe them from the shade of a tree.

The guards were standing there, yawning and complaining about their duties. They were nearly at the end of their shifts, and given that the monsters in Beginnerland were weak outside the wetland, there wasn't much for them to do.

"Wow. So this is what the castle town of a large country looks like," Mako remarked aloud, her eyes sparkling with interest as she gazed at the settlement and the palace beyond the gate.

She'd seen LMAO Castle and its surrounding village when she'd gone to pick up the Hero and had later observed the town of Lafta from the outside. However, Tomorrow Castle was on a different scale, boasting significantly more land and a much larger keep.

Mako's interest was piqued by the greater security as well. Despite the cease-fire currently in effect between humans and demons, her ears bobbed with excitement at the prospect of finding some strong people to tussle with.

"I wonder if this Sunege is in there."

The grand castle towered above the surrounding town from its elevated position. There were scars visible across the entire outer wall—evidence of its sturdiness and the many wars it had likely weathered.

"All right, let's get this over with."

Mako put a little strength into her bestial legs and shot forward with a small *boom* once again.

"*Arrrrrrrgh!*"

The two lazy gatekeepers were suddenly blasted aside, and a clean hole large enough for a person to pass through was gouged into the wooden gate.

Mako ran straight through the castle town without slowing down, covering a two-mile road to the castle portcullis in just ten seconds. When she hit the brakes and looked back behind her, she realized the destruction she had caused. Minitornados were wreaking havoc on the shopping districts and street stalls that she had passed through, sending goods flying into the air on the strong winds.

"Oh, shoot. Sorry, sorry!" Mako apologized, sticking out her tongue in embarrassment. She then turned back to the castle entrance...only to find more chaos.

"Gaaaaah!"

The shock wave that had been kicked up from her sudden stop had sent soldiers soaring upward, and the specially made iron castle doors flew open with a loud groan. This was only a fraction of the might of the strongest member of the Demon Army's Four Demon Generals.

"Th-there are cries in the castle town! Reports say a sudden shock wave traveled through the shopping district, and someone was sighted approaching the castle at high speed!" cried a castle guard after bursting through the door to the throne room.

"That's not all, Your Majesty! Some kind of wind has been surging through the halls and reducing everything it touches to rubble! This likely means that a monster, no, some kind of high demon has breached the castle walls!" proclaimed a panicked combat soldier in heavy armor who had raced into the room after the guard.

"You fools! This is the royal palace! Make sure to bow and address the king properly!" scolded a cabinet minister stationed next to the throne, failing to read the room and fearing his subordinates' behavior would reflect poorly on him. "...Although, if you're that distressed, this must be no small matter," he appended with a somber expression to make up for his outburst.

Everyone gawked at the minister in disbelief. There was no time for all this formality. As was common in modern society, the higher-ups in the castle were quite annoying, expecting decorum even in times of emergency.

"Could it be a demon?! How could you have allowed such a thing to traipse into *my* castle?! What are the guards and soldiers doing?!" bellowed the king.

That's what I just said, the soldier thought in irritation. He stamped his feet, frustrated, wanting the king to go ahead and give his orders to deal with the threat.

"…Oh right! Your Majesty, please flee using the emergency escape route! I believe this to be the vicious assault of a monster, no, a high demon! You can leave this to me, your trusted minister!" the cabinet minister shouted, clearly trying to steal credit from his subordinates by fooling the king into believing he had control of the situation. The guards were beyond fed up with him.

"Hey now, let's calm down, minister. In fact, everyone should. You're repeating the same thing over and over again. I can't tell what anyone is trying to say through your incoherent babble," admonished the King of Tomorrow. He looked dignified atop his throne, wearing a lavish crown and stroking his tremendously long beard. The soldiers were understandably relieved to see their ruler take charge.

"There is no need to fear. Even if a monster has breached the castle walls, Sunege, my son and the second prince of Tomorrow Castle, is here. He has a strange way of speaking, but he is every bit as strong as his reputation," boasted the king.

The guards joyfully voiced their agreement.

"Oh, th-that's right!"

"Sunege works day and night exterminating monsters to sharpen his skill! He's level twenty-five! No monster in Beginnerland is a match for him!"

"He does talk a bit weird, though!"

"He sure does!"

"Right?!"

You don't need to explain my own son's level like you're some no-name NPCs... Also, are they making fun of him? thought the king. It was true that his son had odd speaking patterns, however, so he let that comment slide.

"Oh, hey, guys! How's it going?"

A lovely female voice suddenly echoed in the throne room. Tomorrow Castle was usually occupied almost entirely by men, so the presence of a woman there was unusual. The queen and the princess were currently away, and it was time for the other women in the palace to begin preparing dinner. Not knowing what to think, everyone turned toward the source of the voice.

"Um, is there a prince named Sunege here?" a girl inquired entirely too casually. She had animal ears protruding from her red hair, fur on the back of her hands, and legs that looked just like a beast's.

"D-d-de..."

Her appearance was markedly different from the women whom the gathered humans were used to. It didn't require even a moment to understand what she was.

"Demon!!!"

"A—a humanoid high demon?! Sh-she's gonna kill us!!!!!"

"Eeeeeeek!"

Panic spread through the room like wildfire.

"Everyone, calm down! This is surely some kind of costume!" screamed the cabinet minister.

"There's no way that's a costume! She broke into the castle! Are you blind, you self-serving bureaucrat?!" yelled a soldier in response.

The room descended into a pandemonium of cries and personal insults. The king and everyone else in the room jumped back in fear and pointed their swords and spears at the blank-faced demon with catlike features.

"Aww, you've gotta be kidding, *meow*. You guys realized I'm a demon, right? I thought you wouldn't figure it out because I'm humanoid."

"It's not hard to tell!"

"Those are totally bestial limbs!!"

"What're you doing in this castle?!"

"Honestly, I just want to squish those adorable furry legs!"

Some spoke up with reasonable comments, while others shamelessly voiced their honest desires. The king then cut through the shouting with a calm and authoritative tone.

"H-hey, listen up, everybody. There's no need to fear. Sunege is one of the greatest knights in the entirety of Beginnerland. He will save us all."

Unfortunately, the ruler's visibly shaking legs betrayed his confidence. His boasts had also set the bar quite high for his son.

"Ooh, so this Sunege really is strong! I can't wait to see him," Mako said before placing something she had been holding in one hand down on the red carpet.

"…Hmm?"

When everyone's eyes shifted to that thing, no, *person*, the shocking truth became clear.

"No…"

The person Mako placed on the ground was none other than Sunege, second prince of Tomorrow Castle. He wasn't dead, but he definitely wasn't conscious.

"She defeated Sunegeeeeeeee!!!!!!!"

"Why?!?!?!?!?!?!"

"Whaaaaaat?!?!?!"

Everyone but Mako began to wail in disbelief.

Sunege had led the charge against Mako, as he was the only person in the castle capable of meeting such an assault, yet Mako had knocked him out in an instant.

"Wait, what? This guy is Sunege?" the demon asked.

"…Yes. He's a strange fellow, but that is Sunege, our prince."

"Sunege… Sunny egg… Ha-ha-ha!"

The soldiers began to shout some truly ridiculous things amid their terror, likely as some form of escapism. They knew they couldn't defeat the intruder, and they all hated the cabinet minister, so most of them had pretty much checked out mentally.

"You'll die for what you've done, you filthy demon!!!!" the King of Tomorrow suddenly screamed.

He raised his staff, an ornate rod affixed with extravagant jewels, and threw it at Mako. The girl easily dodged it, then knocked the king out with a karate chop to the head. The cabinet minister collapsed, playing dead. All still watching knew that their nation was finished.

"Man, I'm disappointed Sunege was so weak. Ah, but don't worry. I'm not going to kill anyone. The Hero told me not to," announced Mako.

The demon walked toward Sunege, who was still sprawled out on the floor. Because she had defeated the strongest person currently in the castle (which the soldiers blamed on the cabinet minister), no one moved to stop her.

"Oh, those legs… My heart can't take it…"

The furries among the guards had another reason for backing down; they were too enraptured by how cute she was.

"I really got my hopes up, though. I'll be in a bad mood the rest of the day if I leave without doing anything."

Mako then conceived of the perfect punishment. She stripped Sunege's legs bare and started plucking out their hairs one by one.

"…What in the world?" one soldier uttered aloud. Nobody understood what was going on anymore. The atmosphere of the now-quiet throne room quickly turned surreal.

While a bit of a digression, let's return to the Hero in the wetland. He tried and failed to escape from the kobolds three times. Fortunately, he managed to get away on his fourth attempt. On with the story.

DEMON GENERAL 1
Beast God Mako's betrayal deepens. Now she's following the Hero's direct orders
20:15

DEMON GENERAL 2
What?!
20:16

DEMON GENERAL 3
Read 20:16
This is really, really bad!

DEMON GENERAL 1
Yes
20:16

DEMON GENERAL 1
At this rate, Mako will become his full-fledged pawn, making her the single greatest enemy of the Demon Generals
20:16

DEMON GENERAL 2
No way...
20:16

DEMON GENERAL 3
Read 20:17
Mako is stupid strong...

DEMON GENERAL 1
And super cute...
20:17

DEMON GENERAL 3
Read 20:17
Tbh, I want her to bite me with her fangs

DEMON GENERAL 2
Huh?
20:17

DEMON GENERAL 3
Read 20:18
Huh?

DEMON GENERAL 1
We must form a plan to deal with her
20:15

DEMON GENERAL 2
Agreed
20:16

DEMON GENERAL 3
Read 20:16
"sigh" Fine

NICOLETTA

20:16

NICOLETTA
Read 20:16
There's no need to worry

NICOLETTA
Read 20:17
I, Vampire Queen Nicoletta of the Demon Generals, will neutralize the Hero!

DEMON GENERAL 1
Oh! Nicoletta's got this one?
20:17

DEMON GENERAL 2
We're counting on you!
20:17

DEMON GENERAL 1
But why'd you send a picture of yourself?

NICOLETTA
Read 20:18
I...

NICOLETTA
Read 20:18
sincerely enjoy humiliation!!!!!

☆MAKO☆
I'm back meow
21:05

HERO
Oh, Mako.
Hello
Read 21:06

☆MAKO☆
Wait, what's this group?
21:06

HERO
Ah, about that
Read 21:06

NICOLETTA
Mwahahahaha!!!
21:06

NICOLETTA
Long time no see, Mako!!
21:07

NICOLETTA
It would seem I am also joining the Hero's party!

He kindly added me to the chat!!
21:07

HERO
...Yep, I did
Read 21:07

☆MAKO☆
Ohhh
21:07

☆MAKO☆
She's a masochist tho... It's annoying
21:07

NICOLETTA
Yes! Insult me more...!
21:08

NICOLETTA
And feel free to bite me hard, Mako!!!
21:08

☆MAKO☆
That's gross
21:08

HERO
Oh, how'd it go, Ms. Mako?
Read 21:10

☆MAKO☆
Hmm?
21:10

HERO
You know with that Prince Sunege
Read 21:11

☆MAKO☆
Oh. He didn't even make fur a good workout
21:11

☆MAKO☆
He was incredibly weak

I beat him up and plucked out all his leg hairs
21:12

HERO
Leg hairs?
Read 21:12

NICOLETTA
Hey, wait a sec, Mako
21:12

NICOLETTA
Does that mean if I annoy you enough, you'll
21:12

NICOLETTA
pluck out my leg hairs?
21:12

☆MAKO☆
No way
21:13

NICOLETTA
Please! I'm begging!
21:13

☆MAKO☆
Absolutely not
21:14

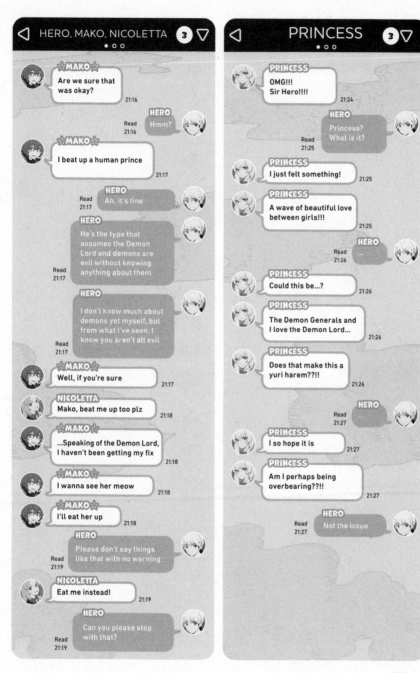

☆MAKO☆
Are we sure that was okay?
21:16

HERO
Read 21:16
Hmm?

☆MAKO☆
I beat up a human prince
21:17

HERO
Read 21:17
Ah, it's fine

HERO
Read 21:17
He's the type that assumes the Demon Lord and demons are evil without knowing anything about them

HERO
Read 21:17
I don't know much about demons yet myself, but from what I've seen, I know you aren't all evil

☆MAKO☆
Well, if you're sure
21:17

NICOLETTA
Mako, beat me up too plz
21:18

☆MAKO☆
...Speaking of the Demon Lord, I haven't been getting my fix
21:18

☆MAKO☆
I wanna see her meow
21:18

☆MAKO☆
I'll eat her up
21:18

HERO
Read 21:19
Please don't say things like that with no warning

NICOLETTA
Eat me instead!
21:19

HERO
Read 21:19
Can you please stop with that?

PRINCESS
OMG!!!
Sir Hero!!!!
21:24

HERO
Read 21:25
Princess? What is it?

PRINCESS
I just felt something!
21:25

PRINCESS
A wave of beautiful love between girls!!!
21:25

HERO
Read 21:26
...

PRINCESS
Could this be...?
21:26

PRINCESS
The Demon Generals and I love the Demon Lord...
21:26

PRINCESS
Does that make this a yuri harem??!!
21:26

HERO
Read 21:27
...

PRINCESS
I so hope it is
21:27

PRINCESS
Am I perhaps being overbearing??!!
21:27

HERO
Read 21:27
Not the issue

YUSUKE NITTA   55

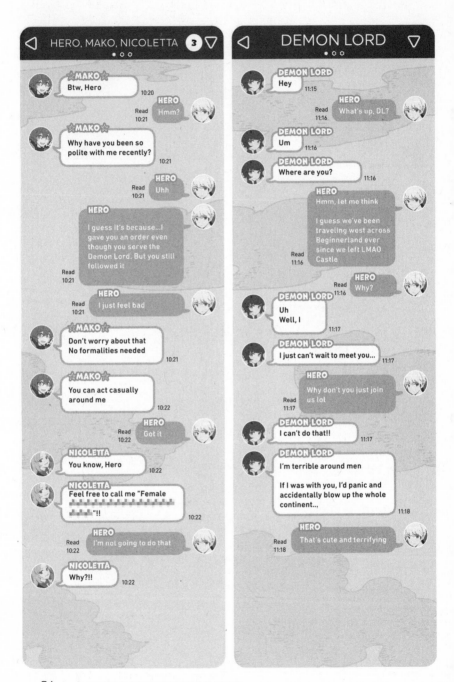

MAKO
Btw, Hero
10:20

HERO
Hmm?
Read 10:21

MAKO
Why have you been so polite with me recently?
10:21

HERO
Uhh
Read 10:21

HERO
I guess it's because...I gave you an order even though you serve the Demon Lord. But you still followed it
Read 10:21

HERO
I just feel bad
Read 10:21

MAKO
Don't worry about that
No formalities needed
10:21

MAKO
You can act casually around me
10:22

HERO
Got it
Read 10:22

NICOLETTA
You know, Hero
10:22

NICOLETTA
Feel free to call me "Female ▦▦▦▦▦"!!
10:22

HERO
I'm not going to do that
Read 10:22

NICOLETTA
Why?!!
10:22

DEMON LORD
Hey
11:15

HERO
What's up, DL?
Read 11:16

DEMON LORD
Um
11:16

DEMON LORD
Where are you?
11:16

HERO
Hmm, let me think

I guess we've been traveling west across Beginnerland ever since we left LMAO Castle
Read 11:16

HERO
Why?
Read 11:16

DEMON LORD
Uh
Well, I
11:17

DEMON LORD
I just can't wait to meet you...
11:17

HERO
Why don't you just join us lol
Read 11:17

DEMON LORD
I can't do that!!
11:17

DEMON LORD
I'm terrible around men

If I was with you, I'd panic and accidentally blow up the whole continent...,
11:18

HERO
That's cute and terrifying
Read 11:18

DEMON LORD
Also, my mom told me something when she was still alive
11:19

Read 11:20 **HERO** What?

DEMON LORD
One day, a hero riding a white stallion would come to seek me out

So I should wait in the castle until then
11:20

DEMON LORD
So yeah...
11:20

Read 11:20 **HERO** I see...

DEMON LORD
Huh?
11:21

Read 11:21 **HERO** Nvm, it's nothing

DEMON LORD
That's why...
11:22

DEMON LORD
I'll wait
11:22

DEMON LORD
I'll wait for you!!!
11:22

Read 11:22 **HERO** Ok lol

DEMON LORD
I'll do my best to get over my fear of men before then!!!
11:23

Read 11:23 **HERO** Ok

Read 12:25 **HERO** Mako

MAKO
Heyo
12:26

HERO
I've wanted to ask you something. Why is the Demon Lord afraid of men?

Read 12:26

MAKO
Hmm, I actually don't know for sure
12:26

MAKO
There is one thing, though

She really, really hates her dad, the Demon Overlord
12:27

HERO
...He didn't abuse her when she was little, did he...?
Read 12:27

MAKO
Oh, no, nothing like that
12:27

MAKO
She's 16 now

But at 5, she was already stronger than her dad
12:27

Read 12:27 **HERO** That's truly terrifying...

NICOLETTA
Abuse is a terrible thing. It is the height of folly for a parent to harm their child
12:28

NICOLETTA
If anyone ever feels that kind of impulse, they can take it out on me
12:28

NICOLETTA
One day, I wish to rule over all pain
12:29

NICOLETTA
As the "Queen of Pain"
12:29

Read 12:29 **HERO** She's beyond saving

YUSUKE NITTA　　57

It was half past four in the morning, and the sun had not yet risen to light the grassy plains of Beginnerland. A sudden sound roused the Hero from sleep.

Before lying down last night, his group had discovered a waterfall not far from their campsite. Now some kind of strange, otherworldly voice was issuing from that direction.

"…What is that bizarre screaming sound?"

It occurred to the Hero that it could have been a rare monster. However, that was unlikely because Mako would have sensed it from her spot in a tree. He then decided he was too tired to deal with whatever it was, wrapped himself up in his sleeping bag, and used the ground and the comforter to plug his ears.

"…"

Unfortunately, he couldn't fall back asleep. The voice sounded less like a monster and more like…the shrill gasps of a girl in pain. It was a little creepy.

"Goddamn it, what is that…?" the Hero muttered to himself.

Reluctantly, he stood, picked up a short sword for defense—knowing he probably wouldn't be able to make good use of it—and headed toward the waterfall.

The voice cut through all other sounds, growing louder as he approached. And what the Hero discovered…

"Ouch! Oof! Ooooh! Yes, yes!"

…was Nicoletta, a member of the Demon Army's Four Demon Generals. The vampire masochist who'd joined his party the other day. She was standing fully clothed under the waterfall and lashing herself with a thorned whip, looking as if she were performing some demented version of morning aerobics.

"What the…?"

Such a sight left the Hero speechless. Even if he had thought of something to say, he wouldn't have been able to get a word in through all the "Yes! Ooooh! That's it! More, more!" coming from Nicoletta.

He watched her for five minutes, ten minutes, but she showed no sign of letting up. The woman then swapped out the whip she had been holding with both hands and began to crack herself incessantly with two lashes at once. *Very* forcefully.

The Hero could do nothing but look on and feel sorry for her as he hid in the shade of a tree.

"Ahhh, that feels good. That feels *sooooo* good!"

Nicoletta was deep in her own little world, and her triumphant expression made it look like she had just won first place in a hundred-meter breaststroke. Her blond hair was wet, and her neat vampire clothes were soaked and growing ragged. Yet her red eyes continued to shine, undaunted.

Looking at her objectively, no one would have batted an eye if you said she seemed like a bathing goddess. "Judging from her appearance alone, she's truly beautiful," the Hero muttered.

"Wha—?!"

Nicoletta turned to stare intently at the shadow the young man was hiding in, as if she had heard his whisper.

"Who's there?! One should be open rather than hide away unseen. What was wrong? I'm not mad—the steam is not shooting out of my ears! I'll forgive you if you give me your best licking."

The Hero had no idea what she was talking about. Her grammar was all over the place. More than anything, her word choice was bizarre. He began to doubt whether she was actually a member of the Demon Generals. She didn't seem like a bad person, but her demeanor was screwing with the Hero's head.

"Not coming out? You're saying I should go to you, and we'll do the licking there? Yes, that must be it!" Nicoletta exclaimed, emerging from the waterfall with a loud splash. The Hero reluctantly left his hiding spot, accepting that escape was impossible.

"Ooh, it was you, Hero. Perfect timing. You caught me during my morning routine. I was hoping someone would come by to crack the whip for me."

Leaving the Hero once again stunned by her nonsensical words, Nicoletta abruptly spread out a case she had left by the side of the waterfall.

"It doesn't have to be a lash. I only have what's on hand, but you can pick any other tool. I really don't mind," she stated.

The Hero wanted to fire back with *When did I agree to torture you?* But given his communication difficulties, all he could do was stare at her in dumbfounded silence.

"Hmm? Ah, you look like you want to say something. Then allow me to introduce myself again. I'm Nicoletta! I'm a vampire and a persistently pushy masochist! I'm a pervert from the slums around the Demon Lord Castle, constantly in pursuit of the greatest pain in history. My morning exercises are meant to heighten my spirit as a masochist."

Even if he'd possessed the confidence to reply, the Hero couldn't think of a retort. *You serve the Demon Lord, so don't call the area around her castle the "slums." Also, your way of speech just totally changed. Be consistent with your personality. This is making my head hurt...* That's when he gave up on thinking.

"...? Ah, that's right. You have trouble speaking, just like the Demon Lord. Though, I think not responding to people can be an excellent strategic move to grab hold of their attention. *Sei d'accordo?*"

Someone help me. I need a translator, thought the Hero.

"Anyway, your arrival must mean that you want to help with my routine. That's wonderful, Hero! Show me a portion of that sadist spirit of yours!" Nicoletta screamed, her voice echoing all around. The Hero had already accepted defeat. He judged that the smartest move would be to say nothing and do as requested.

Just after six in the morning, Mako awoke from atop her branch in the large tree she was sleeping in.

What is that racket? It's so early, she thought. She had been about to dismiss it as Nicoletta's usual nonsense when her ears caught what had to be a second voice mixed in with the first. It warranted investigation.

"I'm so tired..."

She dropped down quietly from the tree and sauntered toward the waterfall, the apparent source of the odd sounds. There, she was then greeted by a scene she could never have imagined.

"What are you doing, Hero?! That's not a vital spot! Hit me right *here*! *Strike! Strike!* Now yell as you hit me!"

"…"

"Together now! And *strike*! And *strike*! Okay, *gender bender fender! Gender bender fender! Snap crackle pop! Choo choo!*"

The Hero was karate chopping Nicoletta according to her instructions. If his expression was any indication, he couldn't believe what he was doing.

"…What am I looking at?" muttered Mako.

It was an excellent question.

HERO
Hey, Mako
Read 16:30

MAKO
? 16:31

HERO
Messaging the Demon Lord made me realize something
Read 16:31

MAKO
Oh? 16:31

HERO
She can be really childish sometimes
Read 16:31

MAKO
Well, she's only 16 16:31

MAKO
She also lived in isolation for 8 years, so she's not great at holding a conversation, meow 16:31

HERO
Huh?
Read 16:32

HERO
What do you mean by the 8 years thing?
Read 16:32

MAKO
Oh, have I not mentioned that? 16:32

MAKO
The Demon Lord lived in the Holy Spring from age 5 to 13 to repress her overwhelming magic power 16:32

HERO
???
Read 16:33

MAKO
IIRC, she entered the Holy Spring soon after her mother died 16:35

MAKO
When the Demon Lord turned 5, she started thinking she wanted to "improve relations with humans" 16:35

HERO
Oh?
Read 16:36

MAKO
But even at that young age, she already held unrivaled magic power

It wasn't safe for her to even talk with humans 16:36

MAKO
Standing near her was enough to disintegrate them 16:36

HERO
Terrifying 5-year-old...
Read 16:36

MAKO
That's why she spent 8 years in the Holy Spring. She wanted to interact with humans directly without harming them 16:36

MAKO
Thanks to that, she was able to repress her power

and meow she's spending time with the Princess no problem 16:37

HERO
Wow
Read 16:37

NICOLETTA
The Demon Lord returned from the Holy Spring 3 years ago
16:38

NICOLETTA
then drove her father into the Down Below
16:38

NICOLETTA
That was what made the cease-fire 3 years ago possible
16:38

HERO
Oh yeah, I saw that on the internet
Read 16:39

HERO
Didn't the Demon Army suddenly withdraw despite having a superior position over the humans?
Read 16:39

NICOLETTA
Yes. We members of the Demon Generals tried to stop her
16:39

NICOLETTA
but it resulted in a dramatic decline in both human and demon deaths
16:39

NICOLETTA
...I'm still not sure if it was the right choice
16:40

NICOLETTA
but it is all thanks to our master that war vanished from the world
16:40

HERO
Wow, Nicoletta...
Read 16:40

HERO
You sound like a normal person
Read 16:41

NICOLETTA
Just what do you think I am?!!
16:41

☆Mako☆ invited ♪Pino♪ to the group.
♪Pino♪ joined the group.

HERO
??
Read 16:43

☆MAKO☆
Sorry for interrupting
16:43

☆MAKO☆
She was begging me to let her into the group...
16:43

♪PINO♪
Mwahahahahaha!!
16:43

♪PINO♪
I am one of the Demon Army's Four Demon Generals, Pino the Fallen Angel!
I hereby join the group chat for the Hero's traveling party!!
16:43

NICOLETTA
Ah, so Pino's here
16:44

☆MAKO☆
Whoooo, meowre annoying peeps (-_-;)
16:44

HERO
Anyway, it's nice to meet you, Pino
Read 16:44

♪PINO♪
D-dummy! I'm not going to be your friend or anything, okay?!
16:44

♪PINO♪
...But if you all insist
16:44

♪PINO♪
I can try to...get along...
16:45

HERO
All right, sounds good to me
Read 16:45

A high demon with ebony wings flapped down to land where the Hero, Mako, and Nicoletta were standing.

Her beautiful long silver hair fluttered in the wind, and her eyes, irises and all, were as black as an abyss. Her expressionless face suggested a coolheaded personality, and her dark clothing covered nearly her entire body. Despite her eye-catching attire, her wings were still the most striking feature.

They were spread wide when she touched down in front of the Hero, but they then quickly shrunk in size thereafter. The Hero, Mako, and Nicoletta stared at the new arrival in silence, and she spoke up in an indifferent voice.

"I am Pino, one of the Demon Army's Four Demon Generals. Nice to meet you."

"..." Given his extreme shyness, the Hero couldn't respond.

"...Pino, what are you doing here? Did our master order you to join us?" asked Mako, voicing the question on everyone's mind.

"N-no, of course not!" Pino hastily replied.

"Okay."

"The Demon Lord did not ask me to do this, okay?!?!"

"She really didn't, huh?"

"Guess not."

Nicoletta's and Mako's answers were dry and unamused. Without any effort at all, the two had seemingly slipped into a comedy routine with Pino.

"S-so I have absolutely zero intention o-of being your friend or anything like that! But if you all insist, then I can try to…get along…"

"You just said almost that exact thing in our group chat."

Mako and Nicoletta were quite antagonistic toward Pino. The pair didn't hate her, but protecting the Demon Lord was their first priority, and they were unsure why Pino had left her side to join them with the Hero. They couldn't help but be on edge.

[Hey, let's all calm down.] Unable to say a word out loud, the Hero tried to ease the tension by sending a group chat message.

"…Anyway, is this the Hero?" inquired Pino, returning to her coolheaded personality and glaring at the young man standing with Mako and Nicoletta.

"Hold on, what's with these abrupt mood swings? Why are you suddenly cool as a cucumber?" asked Mako.

"It's because her personality is a little unstable. Kind of like mine," Nicoletta explained.

"I don't want to hear that from a masochist of all people," quipped Pino.

I wonder if this is how she usually acts. She looks like a calm and intelligent person, thought the Hero. He sent a message to Pino, saying [I agree with you there.]

"You sent me a message? Don't ignore me. I asked if you're the Hero."

"The Hero has an extreme communication disorder. He can only speak through texts," Mako detailed.

"Go easy on him, Pino. He's as shy as I am and a hardcore masochist to boot, so it's not his fault," said Nicoletta.

Mako and Pino ignored Nicoletta's comment, but the Hero nodded in agreement.

"Oh, so you're a masochist, too…," Pino said.

"No, he's not," Mako quickly corrected, helping the shy young man out. The Hero plopped his hand on Mako's shoulder with a self-satisfied grin, appreciative of her understanding. However, Mako hastily rejected the gesture. "Gross!"

"Well, regardless. I'm not acting on the Demon Lord's orders, but I shall join this party as well. I am coming along, and you have no choice in the matter. If he truly bears the human title of 'Hero,' I cannot take him lightly," Pino declared, staring down at the Hero with flaring nostrils. She was the tallest of the Demon Army's Four Demon Generals and the only one in the party the Hero had to look up at to meet her eyes.

"You should know, though, the Hero is stupid cursed and incredibly weak," Mako revealed.

"…Huh?"

"There's really no need to be wary of him. I asked him to inflict pain on me during my morning training the other day, but he was so frail that he ended up healing my body," added Nicoletta.

"You're only saying that because you're a masochist."

"No, really. I'm serious."

As the Demon Generals continued to chitchat, the Hero felt depression settling over him. Even if it was due to the curses, it was unpleasant to have women call him weak, and he felt ashamed.

"...Huh. He really is suffering from numerous heavy curses. A powerful spellcaster must have placed them," Pino remarked.

"That's what we've been trying to tell you," Nicoletta said.

The Hero looked at Nicoletta with a puzzled expression.

"Ah, Mako and I aren't especially skilled at magic, but Pino is a supremely adept sorceress. Undoubtedly, she can see all the details of the curses on you," Nicoletta elaborated, speaking seriously for the first time in a while. The Hero wished she would behave like this all the time.

"Well, it appears I have no choice. I would rather not do this while traveling, but I'll investigate this issue for you, Hero. You could become an enemy of the Demon Lord any day, after all. It is best to be informed about one's foes."

The Hero wasn't certain if Pino was kind or simply meddlesome. Still, despite the coldness of her words, he felt a warmth in her actions.

"That's our Pino!"

"She wasn't named after the Demon Lord's favorite ice cream for nothing."

"Shut up, you two."

Humans fear demons, but these three seem like good people to me, the Hero thought as he watched the trio interact.

If he had set out to travel to the Demon Lord Castle with a group of humans, they probably would have ridiculed him for being useless and kicked him out of the party. He shuddered at the thought. Strange or not, the Hero was grateful for his current situation.

"Ah, but, Hero! D-don't get the wrong idea! I'm not looking into your curses for *your* sake or anything like that! I'm definitely not!" Pino suddenly appended.

Man, is she annoying, mused the Hero.

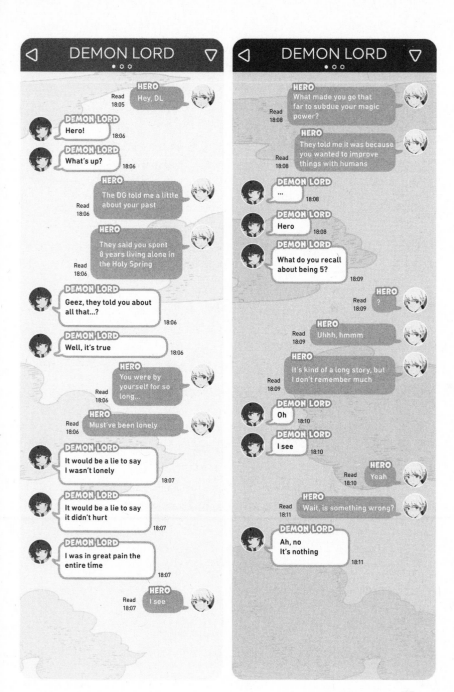

HERO
Hey, DL
Read 18:05

DEMON LORD
Hero!
18:06

DEMON LORD
What's up?
18:06

HERO
The DG told me a little about your past
Read 18:06

HERO
They said you spent 8 years living alone in the Holy Spring
Read 18:06

DEMON LORD
Geez, they told you about all that...?
18:06

DEMON LORD
Well, it's true
18:06

HERO
You were by yourself for so long...
Read 18:06

HERO
Must've been lonely
Read 18:06

DEMON LORD
It would be a lie to say I wasn't lonely
18:07

DEMON LORD
It would be a lie to say it didn't hurt
18:07

DEMON LORD
I was in great pain the entire time
18:07

HERO
I see
Read 18:07

HERO
What made you go that far to subdue your magic power?
Read 18:08

HERO
They told me it was because you wanted to improve things with humans
Read 18:08

DEMON LORD
...
18:08

DEMON LORD
Hero
18:08

DEMON LORD
What do you recall about being 5?
18:09

HERO
?
Read 18:09

HERO
Uhhh, hmmm
Read 18:09

HERO
It's kind of a long story, but I don't remember much
Read 18:09

DEMON LORD
Oh
18:10

DEMON LORD
I see
18:10

HERO
Yeah
Read 18:10

HERO
Wait, is something wrong?
Read 18:11

DEMON LORD
Ah, no
It's nothing
18:11

IF THE RPG WORLD HAD SOCIAL MEDIA...

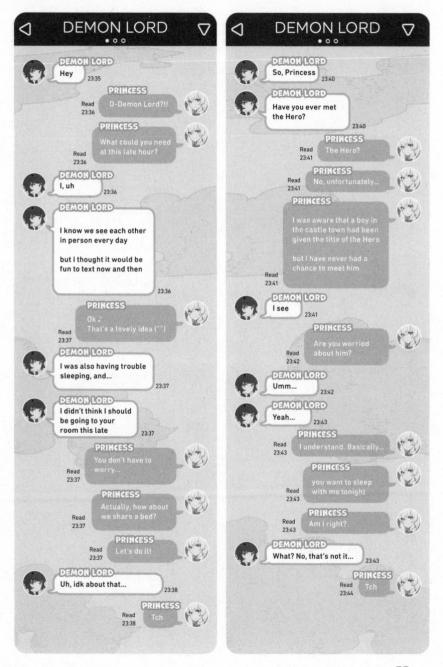

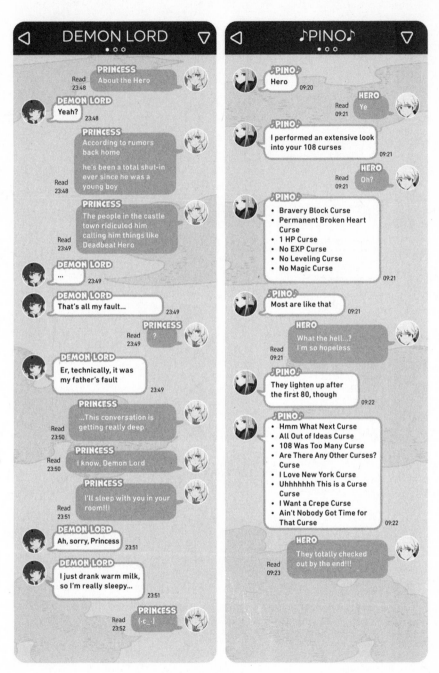

IF THE RPG WORLD HAD SOCIAL MEDIA...

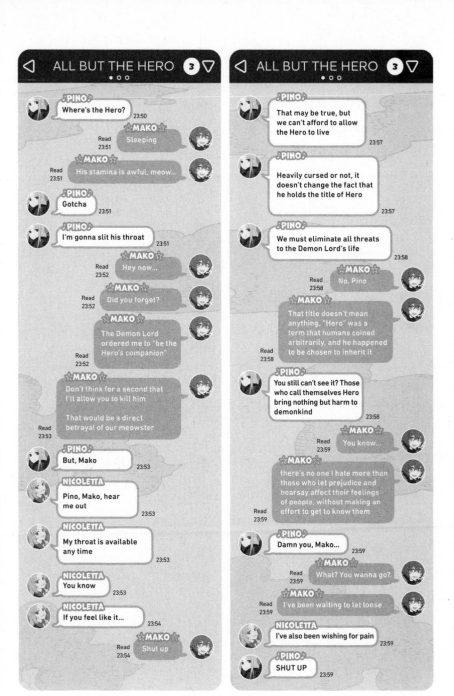

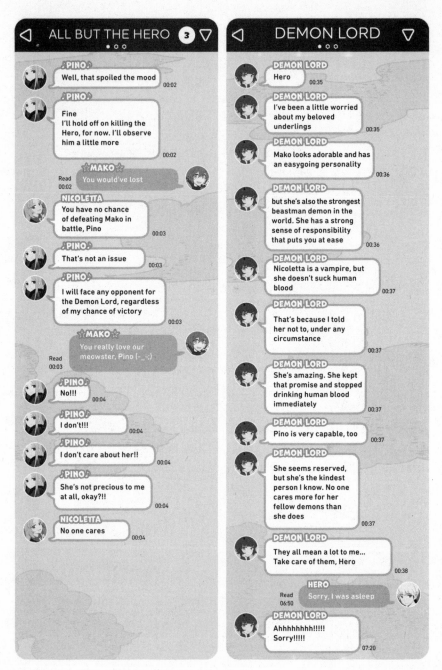

♪PINO♪
Well, that spoiled the mood
00:02

♪PINO♪
Fine
I'll hold off on killing the
Hero, for now. I'll observe
him a little more
00:02

☆MAKO☆
Read
00:02
You would've lost

NICOLETTA
You have no chance
of defeating Mako in
battle, Pino
00:03

♪PINO♪
That's not an issue
00:03

♪PINO♪
I will face any opponent for
the Demon Lord, regardless
of my chance of victory
00:03

☆MAKO☆
Read
00:03
You really love our
meowster, Pino (-_-;)

♪PINO♪
No!!!
00:04

♪PINO♪
I don't!!!
00:04

♪PINO♪
I don't care about her!!
00:04

♪PINO♪
She's not precious to me
at all, okay?!!
00:04

NICOLETTA
No one cares
00:04

DEMON LORD
Hero
00:35

DEMON LORD
I've been a little worried
about my beloved
underlings
00:35

DEMON LORD
Mako looks adorable and has
an easygoing personality
00:36

DEMON LORD
but she's also the strongest
beastman demon in the
world. She has a strong
sense of responsibility
that puts you at ease
00:36

DEMON LORD
Nicoletta is a vampire, but
she doesn't suck human
blood
00:37

DEMON LORD
That's because I told
her not to, under any
circumstance
00:37

DEMON LORD
She's amazing. She kept
that promise and stopped
drinking human blood
immediately
00:37

DEMON LORD
Pino is very capable, too
00:37

DEMON LORD
She seems reserved,
but she's the kindest
person I know. No one
cares more for her
fellow demons than
she does
00:37

DEMON LORD
They all mean a lot to me...
Take care of them, Hero
00:38

HERO
Read
06:50
Sorry, I was asleep

DEMON LORD
Ahhhhhhhh!!!!!
Sorry!!!!!
07:20

The Hero woke up early in the morning, as per usual. He had lived as a shut-in who couldn't talk to people his entire life, and now he was suddenly on a long-distance trip to the Demon Lord Castle. His comfortable bed had been traded for a campfire and sleeping bag, and he traveled in the company of a weirdo who whipped herself every morning. Sound rest was a luxury no longer afforded to him.

Two months had passed since the Hero set out from LMAO Castle Town. The three Demon General members traveled at a leisurely pace to accommodate the Hero's slow gait and lack of stamina. Unfortunately, walking the roads with unfamiliar demons was also proving to be quite mentally draining as well.

Urgh... I want to sleep in my bed... I want some of Mom's soup... I want to play games... I want to surf the internet... I want to do nothing...

Naturally, the things that had brought him joy back home were inaccessible now. Yet on some level, the Hero understood that this wasn't all bad.

He traversed the land with his own two feet, experiencing beautiful scenery in person instead of online. The monster meat that Mako prepared every night was surprisingly delicious, and he was getting on well enough with demons—something he would never have thought was feasible.

All this would've been impossible back in his room. The Hero had always been an indoor person, but now he was starting to wonder if he should have ventured outside sooner.

"You're up early, Hero. Good morning!"

Mako was the first to address the Hero in the morning as he warmed his shivering body by the fire. She yawned as she approached, looking as carefree as ever. The Hero, who was hopelessly shy toward all people regardless of gender, quickly inched away from her.

"Oh right. You can't even greet people without using your phone. I'm getting tired of this, *meow*," Mako grumbled, adding a forced cat sound at the end. The Hero didn't feel right responding with a complaint (even through text), given how much she had done to take care of him throughout the journey. Every night, she slept on high tree branches to keep watch and protect the Hero because he was too incapable of defending himself.

"Good morning."

The next to arrive was the vampire, Nicoletta. Her face was practically glowing with satisfaction; she must have finished her morning whip training already.

"What a beautiful day. And look at that blazing sun! The constant tingling on my body feels so good."

Her flesh sizzled and smoked. Sunlight must have been dangerous for vampires.

[…Doesn't that hurt?] the Hero asked using his phone.

"Don't tell me you don't remember the exact number of times

you've experienced pain in your life!" Nicoletta fired back. Her non-sensical response convinced him to drop his inquiry immediately.

"Looks like everyone is awake," Pino the fallen angel remarked, fluttering down to the ground with her black wings out. The small bags under her eyes suggested she had been circling the skies for some time now.

"Where'd you go, Pino?" asked Mako.

"Nowhere in particular. I simply checked the area to ensure no one was watching us. Given our appearances, any human would be able to tell at a glance that we are high demons," Pino replied.

Although demons and humans had agreed to a cease-fire, not everyone was content to forget past offenses—grudges ran deep. Both sides had been embroiled in conflict for centuries, so there were plenty of humans who hated demons and vice versa.

The temporary peace had only been established because the Demon Army had proposed the idea while poised to utterly destroy the world on the Demon Lord's strength alone. Unquestionably, there were humans waiting vigilantly for the first sign of weakness from their perceived enemy. It would be their signal to attack.

"That said, there isn't a human alive who could prove a match for one of the Demon Generals. Changing the subject—I spotted a human castle about three miles ahead. Is that your hometown, Hero?" asked Pino.

The sudden question flustered the Hero, and he quickly pulled out his smartphone to perform some searching. In the group chat, he replied, [No, that's not where I'm from. That's probably Tomorrow Castle, the largest castle in Beginnerland.]

"Oh, then that means we're close to a human town!" Nicoletta said. She hadn't sucked human blood in years and was probably very excited at the rare opportunity to see humans (other than the Hero, of course).

"Ah, that's where I beat up that Sunege guy. It certainly is a big city," Mako answered, recalling her recent visit. As though a light bulb just turned on in her mind, she raised her hand and exclaimed, "Ooooh! I want to explore a human castle town, *meow*!"

"Noooo!" The Hero moaned out loud, unable to contain himself. Hurriedly, he explained himself via text. [That's obviously a bad idea. People will immediately be able to tell that you're demons. Worst of all, it'll be a shock to see members of the Demon Army's Four Demon Generals in the town. Right, Pino?]

The Hero appealed to Pino directly, as she seemed to be the most reasonable and levelheaded of the three.

"I-it's not like I'm interested or anything, but if it's possible, then seeing the town…is not something I'd want to do one bit!!!" Pino exclaimed, suddenly shifting personalities yet again.

Oh, come on! They all *want to go?*

To his credit, the Hero fought valiantly to dissuade his companions, but their curiosity proved too great. Admittedly, he did find the idea of a real bed appealing. After the group set a few boundaries, they decided to enter Tomorrow Castle Town.

HERO
Ok
Read 11:50

HERO
We made it to Tomorrow Castle
Read 11:50

☆MAKO☆
Yay
11:51

♪PINO♪
Yes
11:51

NICOLETTA
Right

HERO
I know you're all looking forward to entering the castle town
Read 11:52

HERO
Still, please make sure no one realizes you're demons

You'll cause a panic
Read 11:52

☆MAKO☆
Ok
11:52

NICOLETTA
Of course
11:52

♪PINO♪
Obviously
11:53

HERO
First thing's first, Mako should put on a hood
Read 11:53

☆MAKO☆
Why?
11:53

HERO
Are you serious?
Read 11:54

☆MAKO☆
I barely look any different from humans. I don't see the need
11:55

HERO
You have furry cat ears!!!
Read 11:55

HERO
You know most humans don't have cat ears, right?!

They WILL draw attention!!!
Read 11:56

HERO
You're also the one who invaded the castle and beat up the prince!!
Read 11:56

☆MAKO☆
That's true
11:56

☆MAKO☆
I can just deny it tho
11:56

HERO
No way that would work!!!! Conceal your ears, please!!
Read 11:57

♪PINO♪
I'll be fine as is
11:57

HERO
No, you won't!!!!
Read 11:57

HERO
You have giant black wings coming out of your back!!! Those will scare people more than anything!!
Read 11:57

NICOLETTA
I think I'll stroll around town in bondage
11:58

HERO
You obviously can't, you crazy masochist!! Why are you TRYING to stand out?! This isn't some porno! Please just act normal!!!
Read 11:58

YUSUKE NITTA   83

♪PINO♪
I've never seen you send so many messages, Hero
11:58

☆MAKO☆
Do your fingers hurt?
11:59

HERO
Read 11:59
Yes!!!

HERO
But I had no choice! You're not even trying to be discreet!!
Read 11:59

NICOLETTA
Feel free to insult me more...
11:59

HERO
Read 11:59
Shut up, pervert!!

☆MAKO☆
Hey, hey. You don't have to get so worked up over this
11:59

♪PINO♪
Right? If necessary, I can hide my wings with a spell
11:59

HERO
...Please, I'm begging you
I want to rest easy at an inn. Don't screw this up for me
Read 12:00

☆MAKO☆
Mew got it! (^^)
12:00

♪PINO♪
I've never been to a human town before. This is exhilarating
12:00

NICOLETTA
Wouldn't it be grand if this town had a store where I could feel the most agonizing, hellish pain?

A "Pain Emporium"
12:00

NICOLETTA
That'd be nice
12:01

HERO
Read 12:01
There isn't one!!!!

HERO
Read 20:15
Man... I'm so tired

DEMON LORD
Hero?
20:16

DEMON LORD
Is everything okay?
20:16

HERO
Read 20:16
I'm fine lol

HERO
We're in a human town. It's the first time for Mako and the others
Read 20:16

HERO
They split up to explore the shops. Keeping up with them is exhausting
Read 20:16

DEMON LORD
Wow...
20:17

DEMON LORD
Sounds fun
20:17

DEMON LORD
I'm jealous...
20:17

DEMON LORD
I'm jealous!!!!!!
20:17

HERO
Sorry (-_-;)
They really wanted to check out the town and wouldn't take no for an answer
Read 20:17

DEMON LORD
I'M JEALOUS!!!!
20:18

HERO
Yeah, I know lol

We can visit a town after I get to the Demon Lord Castle
Read 20:18

DEMON LORD
Really???!!!!
20:18

DEMON LORD
Yayyyyyyy ☆
I have to pick out an outfit ♪♪
20:18

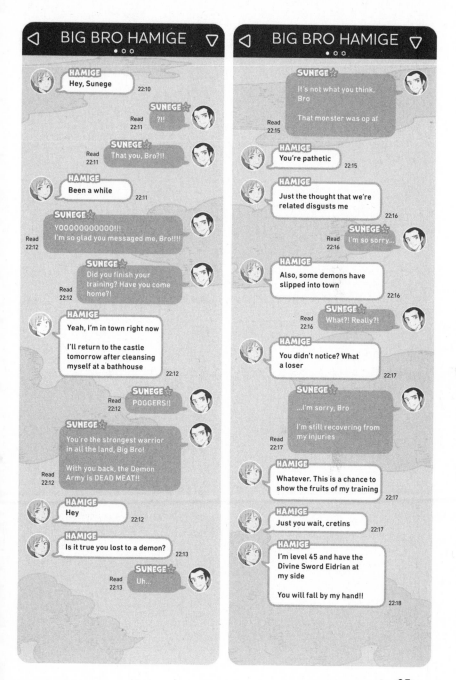

HERO
Good morning, all
Read 08:02

☆MAKO☆
Meowning
08:03

NICOLETTA
I'm sleepy...
08:03

♪PINO♪
Morning
08:03

HERO
How about eating at the inn once we're ready?
Read 08:04

HERO
Remember to hide your cat ears and wings
Read 08:04

☆MAKO☆
Yeah yeah, I know
08:04

NICOLETTA
Pino, will you make it to breakfast?
08:05

♪PINO♪
Don't worry
08:05

HERO
Huh?
Read 08:05

HERO
Did something happen, Pino?
Read 08:06

♪PINO♪
Yeah

Late last night, this guy calling himself the strongest in the land attacked me
08:06

♪PINO♪
We're battling outside town
08:06

HERO
You're texting while fighting?!!
Read 08:07

♪PINO♪
I'm not using my hands
08:08

HERO
During a fight?!!
Read 08:08

♪PINO♪
Going all out would be boring. He wouldn't last a second
08:08

HERO
Wow...
Read 08:09

☆MAKO☆
Oh yeah, some voice's been screaming "EIDRIAN!" since yesterday. It's annoying
08:09

♪PINO♪
I think that's his sword. I broke it after 3 minutes
08:09

HERO
What a blade lol
Read 08:09

NICOLETTA
The inn has pudding, Pino
08:10

♪PINO♪
WHAT??!!!!
08:10

♪PINO♪
I'll finish him right away! Leave some for me!!
08:10

NICOLETTA
Ah, someone just flew by
08:12

☆MAKO☆
Look at him go
08:13

HERO
You don't have to kill him, Pino, just hurry up
Read 08:13

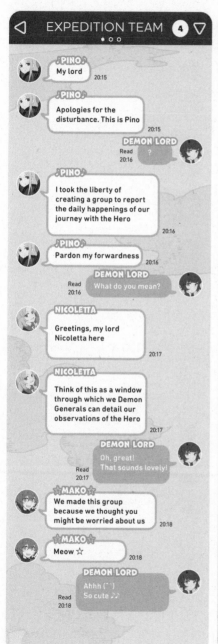

DEMON LORD Btw
Read 20:25

♪PINO♪ What is it?
20:25

DEMON LORD How about the Hero...?
Read 20:26

♪PINO♪ What do you mean?
20:26

DEMON LORD Um
Read 20:26

DEMON LORD Has he said anything about me? Or been worried about me?
Read 20:27

♪PINO♪ ...
20:27

DEMON LORD Ah! Sorry! Forget it!
Read 20:27

NICOLETTA Do you wish to know what the Hero thinks of you, my lord?
20:27

DEMON LORD No! Well, kind of, but...
Read 20:28

DEMON LORD Ahhhh just forget it! Nvm! I'm sorry!!
Read 20:28

☆MAKO☆ I don't know for sure, but
20:28

☆MAKO☆ the Hero is always smiling to himself whenever he messages you, meow
20:28

DEMON LORD !!!!!!!
Read 20:29

DEMON LORD H
21:15

DEMON LORD Hero
21:16

HERO What is it, DL?
Read 21:16

DEMON LORD Umm
21:16

DEMON LORD When you're texting with me, how does it...
21:16

DEMON LORD make you feel?
21:16

HERO ?
Read 21:17

HERO Hmm. Not sure how to put it, but
Read 21:17

HERO it warms my heart
Read 21:17

HERO You're always so kind and considerate of others

I can tell through your messages alone
Read 21:18

DEMON LORD Wasidt
21:19

DEMON LORD li'md
21:19

DEMON LORD I'm burning
21:19

HERO Are you okay?
Read 21:19

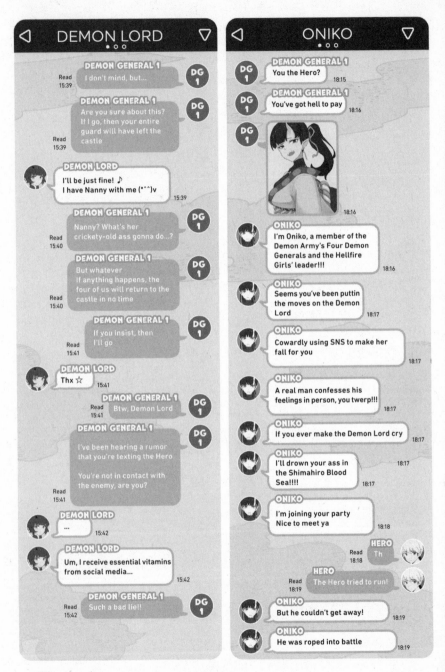

DEMON LORD

DEMON GENERAL 1
I don't mind, but...
Read 15:39

DEMON GENERAL 1
Are you sure about this? If I go, then your entire guard will have left the castle
Read 15:39

DEMON LORD
I'll be just fine! ♪
I have Nanny with me (*^^)v
15:39

DEMON GENERAL 1
Nanny? What's her crickety-old ass gonna do...?
Read 15:40

DEMON GENERAL 1
But whatever
If anything happens, the four of us will return to the castle in no time
Read 15:40

DEMON GENERAL 1
If you insist, then I'll go
Read 15:41

DEMON LORD
Thx ☆
15:41

DEMON GENERAL 1
Btw, Demon Lord
Read 15:41

DEMON GENERAL 1
I've been hearing a rumor that you're texting the Hero
You're not in contact with the enemy, are you?
Read 15:41

DEMON LORD
...
15:42

DEMON LORD
Um, I receive essential vitamins from social media...
15:42

DEMON GENERAL 1
Such a bad lie!!
Read 15:42

ONIKO

DEMON GENERAL 1
You the Hero?
18:15

DEMON GENERAL 1
You've got hell to pay
18:16

18:16

ONIKO
I'm Oniko, a member of the Demon Army's Four Demon Generals and the Hellfire Girls' leader!!!
18:16

ONIKO
Seems you've been puttin the moves on the Demon Lord
18:17

ONIKO
Cowardly using SNS to make her fall for you
18:17

ONIKO
A real man confesses his feelings in person, you twerp!!!
18:17

ONIKO
If you ever make the Demon Lord cry
18:17

ONIKO
I'll drown your ass in the Shimahiro Blood Sea!!!!
18:17

ONIKO
I'm joining your party
Nice to meet ya
18:18

HERO
Th
Read 18:18

HERO
The Hero tried to run!
Read 18:19

ONIKO
But he couldn't get away!
18:19

ONIKO
He was roped into battle
18:19

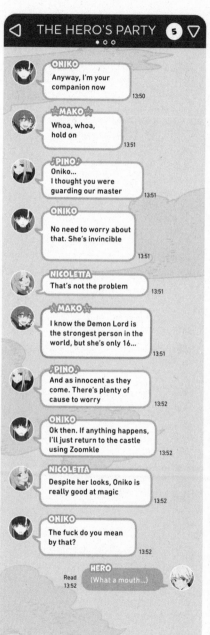

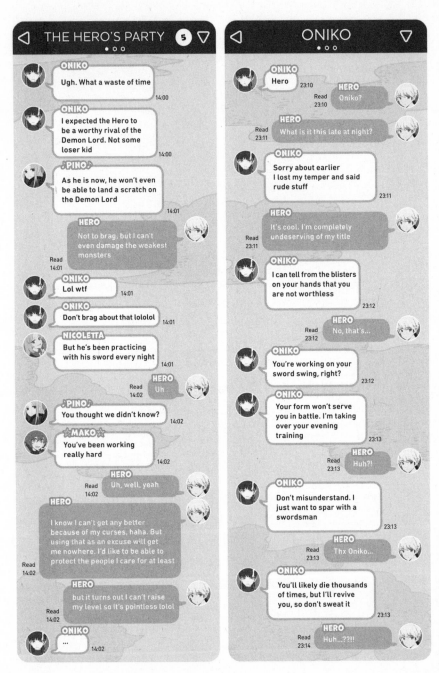

ONIKO
Ugh. What a waste of time
14:00

ONIKO
I expected the Hero to be a worthy rival of the Demon Lord. Not some loser kid
14:00

PINO
As he is now, he won't even be able to land a scratch on the Demon Lord
14:01

HERO
Not to brag, but I can't even damage the weakest monsters
Read 14:01

ONIKO
Lol wtf
14:01

ONIKO
Don't brag about that lololol
14:01

NICOLETTA
But he's been practicing with his sword every night
14:01

HERO
Uh
Read 14:02

PINO
You thought we didn't know?
14:02

MAKO
You've been working really hard
14:02

HERO
Uh, well, yeah
Read 14:02

HERO
I know I can't get any better because of my curses, haha. But using that as an excuse will get me nowhere. I'd like to be able to protect the people I care for at least
Read 14:02

HERO
but it turns out I can't raise my level so it's pointless lolol
Read 14:02

ONIKO
...
14:02

ONIKO
Hero
23:10

HERO
Oniko?
Read 23:10

HERO
What is it this late at night?
Read 23:11

ONIKO
Sorry about earlier I lost my temper and said rude stuff
23:11

HERO
It's cool. I'm completely undeserving of my title
Read 23:11

ONIKO
I can tell from the blisters on your hands that you are not worthless
23:12

HERO
No, that's...
Read 23:12

ONIKO
You're working on your sword swing, right?
23:12

ONIKO
Your form won't serve you in battle. I'm taking over your evening training
23:13

HERO
Huh?!
Read 23:13

ONIKO
Don't misunderstand. I just want to spar with a swordsman
23:13

HERO
Thx Oniko...
Read 23:13

ONIKO
You'll likely die thousands of times, but I'll revive you, so don't sweat it
23:13

HERO
Huh...??!!
Read 23:14

From that day on, the Hero began to train with Oniko, the final member of the Demon Generals to join him. A text just after nine every night was the signal. He was supposed to reach Oniko ten seconds after receiving it.

The Hero was preparing his sleeping bag when he heard the pleasant *ping* sound from his phone, signaling a new message.

"...Ah!"

The blood drained out of his face. The message read, [Come to the nearby watering hole, pronto!]

Spinning around in circles, the Hero desperately tried to recall where the watering hole was.

Activate running motion. Restart zero-second preparation and brain function. Shoot, my body still won't move. Connect directly to modules not under control with artificial heart pump, reconstruct hero body network, update parameters for ignoring meta statements. Feed seems useless, so I'll let that be. Correct deviations in systems responsible for coming up with excuses to give Oniko, goddamn it, connect to exercise routine. My bodily systems are online—my smartphone strap has nothing to do with anything!

Fighting through his panic, the Hero tried his best to get moving. He then lost his temper and screamed.

"Ten seconds is stupid!! This is clearly impossible!!" the Hero cried before hurrying off. A small pool rested southeast of tonight's campsite. It seemed likely that Oniko was waiting there.

"Haaah! Haaah! Haaah!"

Curses had left nearly all of the Hero's stats at zero, so he'd started panting heavily the moment he'd tried to run. Dying was incredibly painful, though, so he'd pushed himself hard, determined not to let it happen this time.

"There you are, Hero."

Oniko was waiting by the pool of water, resting a wooden club on one shoulder. She gave the Hero a kind grin. The Hero got excited, thinking he may have made it on time. Unfortunately...

"*Blargh!!*"

...he received a hit square in the torso from Oniko's cudgel. He had no means of guarding against an attack of such force, so he was sent flying backward about one hundred and fifty feet until he collided into the ground and died.

"...You were slow. That was twenty-two seconds."

As a coffin formed around the Hero, the merciless Oniko took a swig of alcohol from a bottle she had attached to her hip. Face tinged red, she approached the casket.

"*Relife.*"

Oniko chanted a revival spell. The coffin was enveloped in holy light, and the Hero came back to life.

"*Gack!* Did I die?! Why?!"

The memories one had after revival could be a little disorderly. People tended to treat death relatively lightly in this world because of resurrection spells, but injuries to the body still remained. After perishing, a person would lose consciousness, and their body and soul would be separated and confined within a coffin. If one lost their body or soul, revival spells wouldn't work anymore.

The Hero knew that Oniko was the one who restored him, but he'd never even seen the club coming, so it was tough to grasp the situation.

"I told you to get here within ten seconds, you wuss! How the hell do you think you're going to get stronger if you can't even manage that?!" Oniko scolded angrily in her usual foulmouthed manner. "Ready your sword!" she commanded, lifting her club above her head.

Wait, Oniko. Please listen to me. Reaching you within ten seconds after seeing your message is utterly impossible for me. Wait, is this some kind of jock thing? If I had gone to school, I definitely would not have joined any sports clubs. This isn't really my element.

The Hero wanted to say all that and more, but Oniko undoubtedly would've told him to man up before killing him again. The odds of her knowing what school was seemed low, too. Most of all, the Hero could only talk through texts, so his entire internal dialogue was pointless.

"Ready your goddamn sword!" Oniko roared, her patience wearing thin.

Terrified, the Hero quickly grabbed his weapon and held it in front of him. However, after deciding he would be killed immediately because he couldn't stop his shaking, he raised his hand to ask for a time-out.

"…Huh? What is it?" inquired Oniko.

The Hero took out his smartphone and quickly typed out a message.

[Can you please calm down for a second?]

"…I am calm."

[We need to talk.]

"About what?"

[…Can we please drop the ten-second rule? I'm telling you, it's actually impossible. Really. It takes me five seconds just to look at my phone, and it's physically impossible for me to get to the training site after that.]

"You serious?"

[Yes.]

"Then next time, get here within five seconds."

[What the hell?!! That's even less!! You really are a demon, aren't you?!]

"Uh, yeah. I am."

That she was.

"*Hiyaah!*" Oniko suddenly screamed, delivering a clean hit to the Hero's face with her club. A coffin once again appeared out of nowhere around his corpse, and Oniko revived him again.

"*Urghhh…*"

As should not be surprising, dying twice in rapid succession was very painful both physically and mentally. Consider this analogy: It was as if he was simultaneously experiencing intense sunburn and extreme muscular pain throughout his entire body, while also feeling ready to puke from seasickness. He was brought back to life sobbing and deathly pale.

"I heard from Pino that you have a curse that prevents you from gaining experience, even after fighting. That means you can't raise your level. All that leaves is working on your skills and sharpening your feel for battle."

Oniko smashed the ground in front of the staggering Hero, and he stood up straight.

Given his personality, one might have expected him to quit and head to sleep, but something within him must have started to change. He had caused quite a lot of trouble for his parents, and people had always called him the "No-Good Hero." However, meeting the Demon Lord, the Demon Generals, and everyone else he had encountered on this journey had sparked a particular thought in his mind.

This trip has been rough, but some great people have helped me along the way... I might not be a real hero, but...I want to get at least a little stronger.

The young man hadn't lied when he'd admitted his desire to protect the people he cared about. It was an embarrassing thing to say, so he'd passed it off as a joke, yet he honestly had come to feel that way during his time with the Demon Generals.

"...!"

The Hero shook himself, readied his practice sword, and faced Oniko with a determined expression.

"...I like that look in your eyes. That's what I want. This time, you come at me," Oniko instructed, flashing him an abrupt smile.

After a brief pause, the Hero found his resolve and sent a message saying [Understood! I'll give it my all!]

Within ten seconds, however, he was dead for the third time that night.

Pino spread her wings wide and landed quietly next to Mako, who was lazing on a tree branch and watching the Hero as he trained.

"Practicing again, I see," Pino remarked.

"Yeah. He's taking a vicious beating, though. He's dying over and over again," answered Mako.

Unwilling to participate themselves, they both observed the Hero and Oniko.

Revival spells had a time window to them. If they weren't cast quickly enough, the coffin would disappear, and the person inside would be dead for good. Mako and Pino were watching carefully to ensure that didn't happen. They feared that if the Hero were to perish, the kind and gentle-natured Demon Lord would be overcome by rage and lay waste to the world.

"You know, there's something about this that is really bothering me," said Nicoletta the extreme masochist, joining Mako and Pino on the branch. "Why won't Oniko give *me* a vicious beating?" she continued with evident jealousy.

Mako and Pino ignored her.

"I wonder who could have put all those curses on the Hero," Pino thought aloud.

"Who can say? What we can be sure of, though, is that it wasn't our meowster," responded Mako.

"It was someone who possessed considerable power, though, correct? Hmm… I can't field a guess, but what I do know is that I want them to inflict a curse on me that magnifies pain tenfold," Nicoletta stated.

The three of them enjoyed a casual conversation while the deadly sparring continued below.

The Hero had already met his end over five times. Yet, as if riding a high on showing some effort for the first time in his life, he charged resolutely at Oniko every time he was resurrected. Oniko looked pleased to see the Hero devoting himself to his training.

"…Well, it looks like Oniko is having fun. We can probably leave them be for meow," remarked Mako.

"She's always been a natural leader. Having a pupil train so earnestly can't be an unpleasant experience for her," Pino added.

"Okay. Then we'll leave the Hero to Oniko, freeing up the two of you to give me a vicious beating full of love, right?" Nicoletta gave an invitation with a triumphant expression.

"…No, we're not doing that."

"Where did you get that idea from?"

"Honestly, I haven't been feeling very well lately. And I've given it a lot of thought. It's probably because I haven't been receiving enough agony. You know what I'm saying? Punch me, Mako!"

"Shut up already!"

Nicoletta snuggled up to Mako, who kicked her away in irritation. Sadly, the three demons were completely oblivious to the trouble that was about to occur.

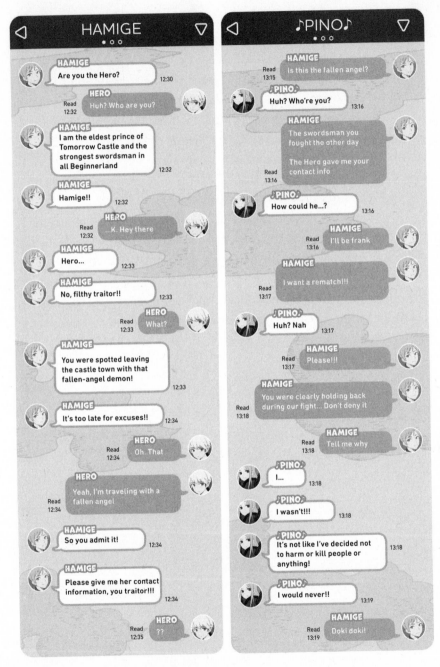

IF THE RPG WORLD HAD SOCIAL MEDIA...

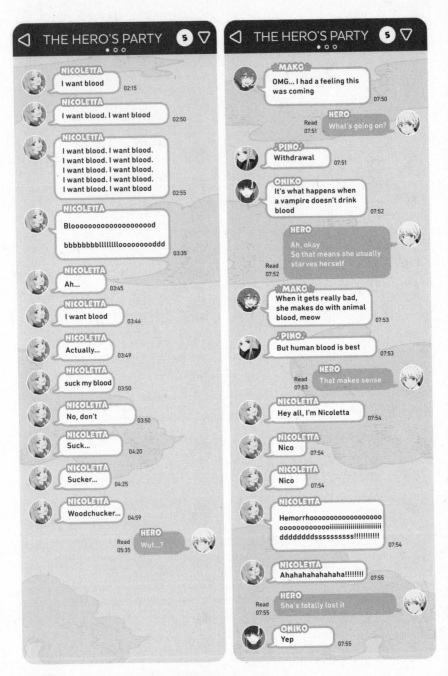

NICOLETTA
I want blood
02:15

NICOLETTA
I want blood. I want blood
02:50

NICOLETTA
I want blood. I want blood.
I want blood. I want blood.
I want blood. I want blood.
I want blood. I want blood
02:55

NICOLETTA
Bloooooooooooooooooooood

bbbbbbbbllllllloooooooodd
03:35

NICOLETTA
Ah...
03:45

NICOLETTA
I want blood
03:46

NICOLETTA
Actually...
03:49

NICOLETTA
suck my blood
03:50

NICOLETTA
No, don't
03:50

NICOLETTA
Suck...
04:20

NICOLETTA
Sucker...
04:25

NICOLETTA
Woodchucker...
04:59

HERO
Wut...?
Read 05:35

MAKO
OMG... I had a feeling this was coming
07:50

HERO
What's going on?
Read 07:51

PINO
Withdrawal
07:51

ONIKO
It's what happens when a vampire doesn't drink blood
07:52

HERO
Ah, okay
So that means she usually starves herself
Read 07:52

MAKO
When it gets really bad, she makes do with animal blood, meow
07:53

PINO
But human blood is best
07:53

HERO
That makes sense
Read 07:53

NICOLETTA
Hey all, I'm Nicoletta
07:54

NICOLETTA
Nico
07:54

NICOLETTA
Nico
07:54

NICOLETTA
Hemorrhoooooooooooooooooooo oooooooooooiiiiiiiiiiiiiiiiiiiiiii ddddddddssssssssss!!!!!!!!!!
07:54

NICOLETTA
Ahahahahahahaha!!!!!!!!
07:55

HERO
She's totally lost it
Read 07:55

ONIKO
Yep
07:55

HERO
You can have some of my blood if you want. I don't mind
Read 08:15

NICOLETTA
???!!!
08:15

NICOLETTA
Srsly????!!!
08:16

PINO
Bad idea. Human blood causes her to enter an aroused state. She'll run wild
08:16

ONIKO
Only the Demon Lord is capable of stopping her then
08:16

HERO
Really?! Not even Mako?
Read 08:16

MAKO
Cat's right
08:16

MAKO
Technically, it's more annoying than difficult
08:17

MAKO
The more damage I inflict, the happier she gets
08:17

HERO
That's actually horrifying...
Read 08:17

NICOLETTA
AHHHHHHHHHHH I WANT BLOOOOOOOOOOOOD!!!
08:17

NICOLETTA
WRYYYYYYYYYY !!!!!!!!!
08:18

HERO
What do we do?
Read 08:19

MAKO
I got this
08:19

MAKO
This'll do it
10:20

10:20

HERO
I suddenly feel all warm and fuzzy!!!
Read 10:21

HERO
What is this?
Read 10:21

PINO
With simple affection
10:21

ONIKO
Bruised and beaten
10:21

HERO
Lolwut Nicoletta, are you okay?
Read 10:21

NICOLETTA
Whew...
10:22

NICOLETTA
I feel so refreshed
10:22

NICOLETTA
as if I were wearing new panties on a holiday morning
10:22

NICOLETTA
and feeling supreme pain as my entire body suffers from the intense heat of the beautiful sun...
10:22

HERO
Thank goodness
She's back to normal
Read 10:22

YUSUKE NITTA 103

HERO Read 14:10
Man...

HERO Read 14:11
We've finally arrived at Nextland

PINO 14:11
How many months has it been?

ONIKO 14:11
We have to move at a snail's pace for the Hero

MAKO 14:11
It's so hot here...

HERO Read 14:12
It's one big desert

ONIKO 14:12
Must be hell for Mako, with all her fur

NICOLETTA 14:12
My entire body burns ferociously from the rays of the sun

NICOLETTA 14:13
but I welcome the suffering!!!!!

HERO Read 14:13
Cool story

HERO Read 14:13
Ok, let's get marching through the sand!

MAKO 14:13
Kay

PINO 14:13
Let's go

HAMIGE 14:13
Indeed

HERO Read 14:13
Wait

MAKO 14:14
Huh

PINO 14:14
What is it, Hero?

HERO Read 14:14
Uh, well, huh?

HERO Read 14:15
I feel some kind of strange presence...

MAKO 14:15
You mean Nicoletta?

HERO Read 14:15
No, different kind of strange

NICOLETTA 14:15
Hey, take that back

HAMIGE 14:16
The heat must be getting to your head, Hero

PINO 14:16
Yeah

HERO Read 14:16
There it is again!!!

HERO Read 14:16
Something is definitely off here!!!!!

HERO Read 14:16
Don't give me that "yeah," Pino!!

HERO Read 14:17
Is Hamige in the group?!!

PINO 14:17
I don't know what you're trying to say

HERO Read 14:17
LIAR!!!!!

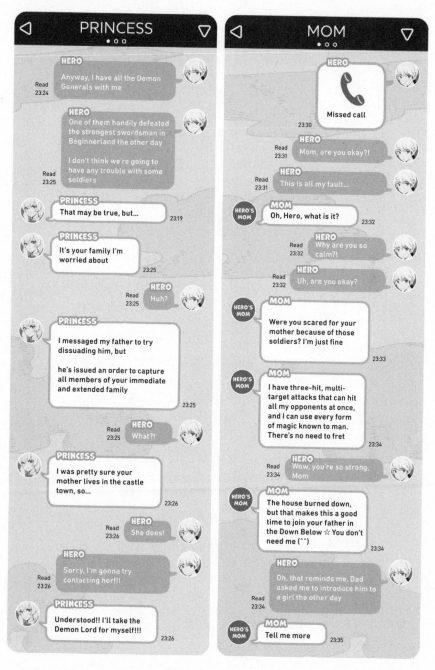

Mamasu, the Hero's mother, was enraged. Clearly, she needed to interrogate her lousy wretch of a husband and get him to spill his guts about this adultery.

She was standing in a grassy field some number of miles from LMAO Castle Town when she placed her tightly balled fists on her waist and unleashed her power.

"Haaaaahh!!!"

A powerful energy that appeared to be some kind of fighting spirit flowed from the woman's body, and her beautiful black hair immediately turned golden. She had gone through what many might refer to as Super…Something.

"…That bastard…," Mamasu muttered in a fierce tone, her usually kind eyes looking like they were out for blood. Her smartphone screen cracked, unable to withstand the energy flowing out of her.

"E-eeeek!"

Five pursuing soldiers from LMAO Castle discovered her in her transformed state. It was evident at a glance how terrifyingly mighty she was, and one of them fell to the ground and wet his pants.

"Don't worry. I ain't gonna hurt y'all," the Hero's mother said, her anger drawing out what may have been a hometown dialect. This rage was not directed at the sortied warriors, however. "My house was razed, but I don't especially care. My insurance will cover it once the Hero is proven innocent."

The structure was a fifty-year-old rental home. The Hero's mother had already been talking about having it rebuilt, so she honestly didn't mind that it had been torched. It was pretty convenient for her.

"You were the one who burned—!"

One of the soldiers started speaking, and then the Hero's mother disappeared. Well, *disappeared* wasn't quite right; what she actually did was circle behind the soldier so quickly that the naked eye couldn't follow the action. It may as well have been teleportation.

"…Wanna finish that sentence?" she whispered into the man's ear.

The soldier shuddered. Goose bumps formed on his entire body, and he dropped to his knees, quivering in fear. If he opened his mouth, he was finished.

"That's right. Now you take care of your family, okay?" Mamasu instructed as she looked down upon the man. While the words themselves were kind, the same could not be said for her eyes, nor her tone.

None could deny that the Hero's abode had burned to the ground. However, it was Mamasu herself who did the deed to make herself look like a victim—allegedly.

"Urrrgh…"

The other soldiers who had been dispatched to the house wanted to scream, *The place blew up before we even did anything!* Yet they knew to hold their tongues.

"You're a good kid. That's right. You've done nothing wrong," the Hero's mom said.

She then floated gently in the air. The soldiers all gazed at her like kids watching a parent leave for a business trip. It wasn't like they could do anything else.

"At one point in time, the phrase *cheating is part of our culture* was prevalent in society. But that is nothing more than a man's excuse. It's arrogant, slothful, and a despicable justification for their desires."

Mamasu looked like a descending god. She didn't look at the soldiers as she spoke, instead appearing as if she were addressing someone far, far away. The warriors from the castle were able to infer that her husband must be two-timing. However, given that he was in the Down Below, a world made up only of males, the truth was that he couldn't have cheated even if he'd wanted to.

"Oh well. I'll have to confirm this by myself," muttered Mamasu, opening her eyes wide. "*I'm angry with you, darling!!*"

Another wave of energy surged around the woman before she sped off into the sky with incredible speed. The exact mechanics behind it were unclear, but she was undoubtedly flying.

The soldiers watched her go.

"…I wonder if this is about her husband."

"…Mostly likely."

"RIP to him."

"Yep."

"Wanna head back?"

"…Yeah. No point in remaining here."

"Wait, hold on… Is it raining?" asked the soldier who was still collapsed on the ground.

"Rain? I don't remember any…"

"No, I—"

It definitely wasn't raining, but the man who'd wet himself desperately wished that it was.

"You know what, I think it was raining."

"…Sure was."

Feeling sympathetic, the others decided to play along.

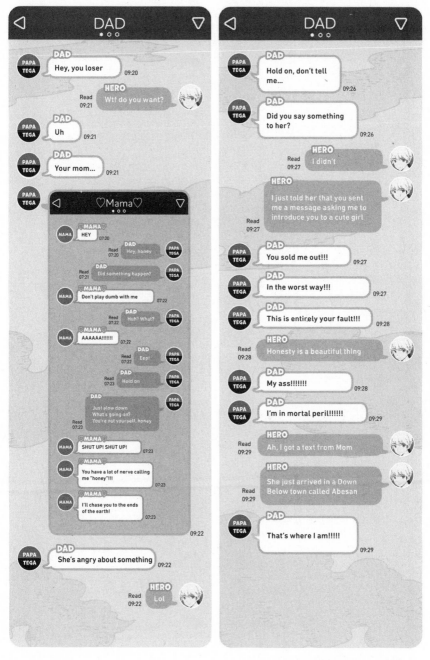

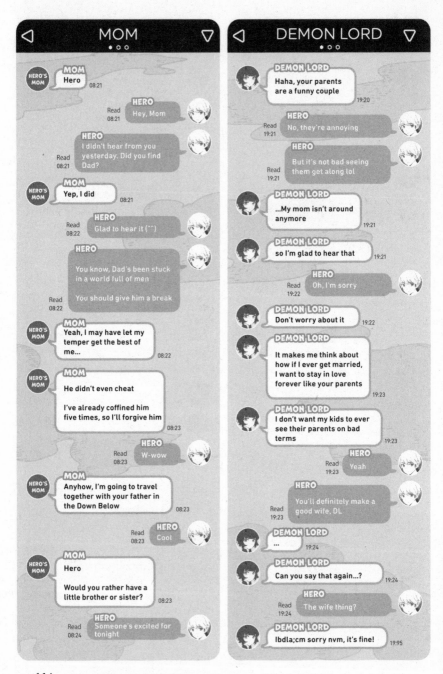

MAKO
Morning, all! 08:15

PINO
Morning 08:15

NICOLETTA
Yes, morning 08:16

PINO
I don't know how to feel about getting used to greeting you all over SNS 08:16

MAKO
We don't have a choice. The Hero still can't talk to us 08:17

PINO
But he's training with Oniko every single night 08:17

PINO
You'd think he would be comfortable with us 08:17

MAKO
I guess 08:17

NICOLETTA
I wish the Hero would reach out to me more readily 08:18

NICOLETTA
with swords, whips, and candles 08:18

MAKO
Yeah, yeah. Die 08:18

ONIKO
Sorry, guys, have a sec? 08:18

MAKO
Hmm? 08:18

ONIKO
The Hero isn't getting up... 08:19

PINO
Huh? 08:19

MAKO
Oniko 08:32

ONIKO
Yes? 08:32

MAKO
The Hero is clearly dead 08:33

ONIKO
...He looks so peaceful 08:33

ONIKO
He must be dead 08:33

MAKO
I said that 08:33

NICOLETTA
Just revive him lolol 08:34

PINO
You're the only one here who can use Relife 08:34

ONIKO
About that... 08:34

ONIKO
I was drinking last night during our training session, and I kinda ended up passing out after killing him 08:34

MAKO
K 08:34

ONIKO
I think it's been too long to resurrect him 08:35

ONIKO
so I can't bring him back 08:35

ONIKO
:p 08:35

MAKO
This is serious!!!!!!!! 08:35

MAKO
What do we do?!!
08:40

MAKO
The Demon Lord will be furious!!!!
08:40

ONIKO
Please don't scream as you type...
My head is pounding from last night...
08:41

NICOLETTA
This is seriously bad, Oniko
08:41

PINO
Once the Demon Lord learns of this, she may destroy the world...
08:41

MAKO
ONIKO!!!!!!!!!!!!!
08:42

ONIKO
I know, I know. Stop screaming
08:42

ONIKO
Hmmm, if we don't do something, he'll be gone for good
I'll borrow some magic power from the boss
08:42

ONIKO
Doing that should allow me to use the most advanced version of Relife
08:43

NICOLETTA
Sounds fine, but...
08:43

PINO
How will you explain this to her?
08:43

ONIKO
I'll say he has a bad cold
08:43

MAKO
Like she'd believe that!!!!
08:44

HERO
It's already evening?!
Read 18:15

HERO
Sorry I didn't answer you yesterday, DL
Read 18:15

DEMON LORD
Don't worry about it ♪
18:15

DEMON LORD
I'm sure you were feeling really terrible with that cold...
18:16

HERO
Cold?
Read 18:16

HERO
(Did I catch a cold...?)
Read 18:16

DEMON LORD
Btw, Hero
18:16

DEMON LORD
how do you feel?
18:16

HERO
Huh?
Read 18:16

HERO
Uhh, hmmm
Read 18:17

HERO
Nice and warm
Read 18:17

DEMON LORD
(//▽//)(//▽//)(//▽//) Hehe
18:17

HERO
What?
Read 18:18

DEMON LORD
I filled the magic power I gave Oniko with lots of love
18:18

DEMON LORD
So...
18:18

DEMON LORD
AHHHH (*/▽*)
18:18

HERO
Huh? What?
Read 18:18

HERO
Come on
Read 15:29

HERO
I really mean it. I think it's important for people to spend time together naked
Read 15:29

HERO
Yep
Read 15:29

NICOLETTA
No "yep" lol
15:29

PINO
You're such a pervert!!!!
15:29

MAKO
I can't wait any longer. I'm getting in
15:30

HERO
Great
I'll be right there, Mako!!
Read 15:30

ONIKO
You seriously need to cool it lol
15:30

PINO
Oniko, let's coffin him
15:31

ONIKO
Good idea
15:31

HERO
I'm sorry, I went too far
Dying really hurts, so please forget I said any of that. I'll back off, so please don't kill me
Read 15:31

NICOLETTA
Sorry, Hero
15:31

NICOLETTA
I thought what you said was interesting. I reported it all to the Demon Lord
15:31

HERO
What?
Read 15:31

HERO
What?
Read 15:31

DEMON LORD
....
....
....
....
....
....
....
....
....
....
15:48

DEMON LORD
....
....
....
....
....
....
....
....
....
15:48

HERO
W-wait, DL!!
Read 15:49

DEMON LORD
...Well...
15:49

DEMON LORD
You are a boy, so I can't blame you
15:49

DEMON LORD
but this is the face I'm making now
15:49

15:50

HERO
I'm sorry, I'll never do it again!!!!
Read 15:50

A loud splash issued from the waters of the oasis.

"Ahh… That feels so good…"

Mako had jumped into the lake fully clothed. While considered the strongest of the Demon Generals, she was no match for the heat of this desert. The fur on her legs and the back of her hands made managing her body temperature in a warm climate difficult. Walking in the desert had been like trekking through a massive sauna. Soaking in the cool water finally stopped her brain from feeling like it was melting.

"Hot damn, this is it right here. It feels incredible."

The next one to enter the pool was Oniko, the ogre monster from Shimahiro. She'd been faring better in the sun than Mako, but that didn't mean the temperature was comfortable for her. A nice break in the oasis was perfect.

"Unbelievable… You two just dived right into a naturally formed lake in the middle of a desert. It's probably full of germs," Pino remarked as she slowly dipped herself into the water.

"It's fine. I purified the lake with magic before we got in, so it's totally clean," responded Oniko.

"I trust your abilities, Oniko. I'm just saying this is careless," Pino answered.

"Oh, it doesn't matter. I was about to collapse out there. Thanks, Oniko," said Mako.

Their moment of peace was then interrupted by a certain someone yelling in the lake.

"*Yoo-hoo*, I'm over here! Catch me if you can, ah-ha-ha-ha-ha!" Nicoletta screamed, racing around in the water. The others paid no mind to her attempts at garnering their attention.

"Well, how often can we enjoy a giant lake like this? Let's have some fun!" exclaimed Oniko, who had until then only submerged the bottom half of her body. She scooped up some water with her hands and then squirted it directly into Pino's face. Pino, who didn't want to get her hair wet, glared at the other demon.

"You mad?"

"You mad?"

Mako and Oniko both taunted her with wide grins on their faces.

"...I'm not angry."

"Oh?"

"But I feel a fire burning within me."

"That sounds like you're ma—"

Before Mako finished her sentence, Pino used magic to manipulate the water to form a giant cannon, then fired it at Mako and Oniko. It was powerful enough that they would've lost some HP had they not been members of the Demon Generals.

"Hold on, if you're going to use water magic, can you use it to perform water torture on me?!" the masochist yelled, finally dropping her previous ploy for attention and joining the others in pursuit of pain.

As the quartet of demon women messed around in a questionably friendly manner, a boy sat on a corner of the lake looking very anxious.

The Hero was sending messages and apologizing profusely to the Demon Lord, bowing his head repeatedly in real life as he did so, even though they weren't yet a couple. It was quite a sad sight.

Even the sun appeared to chuckle sympathetically as it peered down upon the Hero.

PRINCESS
Sir Hero 18:50

PRINCESS
I heard the news 18:50

HERO
Read 18:51 What?

PRINCESS
It sounds like you and the Demon Lord fought 18:51

HERO
Read 18:51 Well, I don't know if I'd call it a fight...lol

HERO
Read 18:51 I apologized for my behavior, so she forgave me

PRINCESS
That simply won't do 18:51

PRINCESS
You need to argue more 18:51

HERO
Read 18:51 Huh? Lol. Why?

PRINCESS
I'm going to help the heartbroken Demon Lord 18:51

PRINCESS
That will be the start of our love affair 18:52

PRINCESS
We'll gain the DG's blessing 18:52

PRINCESS
and we'll celebrate our yuri love 18:52

PRINCESS
Got it? 18:52

HERO
Read 18:52 Uhhhh, no thanks, I'm good

PRINCESS
Dammit 18:55

PRINCESS
I'm so depressed 18:55

HERO
Read 18:56 Lol. What's with the language? It doesn't sound like you

PRINCESS
I can't help it. Look at this 18:56

18:56

PRINCESS
I took this stunning picture of her earlier when she was texting you 18:56

HERO
Read 18:56 (So happy)

HERO
Read 18:57 (So cute)

PRINCESS
(I know) 18:57

PRINCESS
Oops 18:57

PRINCESS
(This girl is mine) 18:57

HERO
Read 18:57 (Shut up)

PRINCESS
There's something I still don't get — 19:01

HERO
Read 19:02 — What?

PRINCESS
You and the Demon Lord have never met, correct? — 19:02

HERO
Read 19:02 — Uh, yeah, that's right

HERO
Read 19:02 — You were the one who connected me with her over SNS, right?

PRINCESS
That's true... — 19:02

PRINCESS
and the Demon Lord talks about you as if she's known you for years — 19:03

HERO
Read 19:03 — ...Hmm, I don't remember ever meeting her

HERO
Read 19:03 — Oh yeah, do you mind if I share that picture with the DG? It seems like they've been suffering lately from a lack of DL

PRINCESS
Please go ahead — 19:03

PRINCESS
I have a full-body pic, too. Do you want that? — 19:04

HERO
Read 19:04 — Really?! Yes!

PRINCESS
I edited it to make her look like a boy, though — 19:04

HERO
Read 19:05 — Keep it

Read 19:25

NICOLETTA
Uh wha, huuuuh??!!! — 19:25

PINO
WHERE THE YOU DIS YOUD FSDJKLFASDJFKLSD; FCMDSCD? WHAA YYY??!! — 19:26

MAKO
WOOOOOOOOOOOOOOOOOOWWWWWWWWWW

HERO
Read 19:26 — Calm down lol. You're breaking the chat

ONIKO
Heyy Heli wherd yoou gett thos?!! — 19:27

HERO
Read 19:27 — The Princess took it

HERO
Read 19:27 — I've got a leg pic, too

Read 19:27

MAKO
AHHHHHHHHHHHHHHHHHHHHHHHHHHHH

PINO
Mako, calm doAHHHHHHHHHHHHHHHHHHH

HERO
Huh?
Do you have a little sister, Nicoletta?
Read 18:20

NICOLETTA
Yes
18:21

NICOLETTA
She's timid, though, so she barely ever goes outside
18:21

HERO
Wow, so she's a shut-in, too
Read 18:21

✿MAKO✿
But she's totally normeow compared with Nicoletta
18:22

♪PINO♪
She's fine compared with Nicoletta
18:22

ONIKO
She's not too weird compared with Nicoletta
18:22

HERO
Nicoletta is not exactly a good point of reference for normalcy!!!
Read 18:22

NICOLETTA
Will you all stop roasting me? That hurts my feelings
18:23

NICOLETTA
but
18:23

NICOLETTA
I love it! Give me more!!!
18:23

HERO
There it is
Read 18:23

♪PINO♪
Right on time
18:24

HERO
What's she like? Is she in the Demon Lord Castle?
Read 18:25

NICOLETTA
No, she lives in the estate I grew up in with my vampire family
18:25

NICOLETTA

18:26

NICOLETTA
Her name is Cass
18:26

HERO
Wow, she's adorable
Read 18:27

✿MAKO✿
Cute compared with Nicoletta, I guess
18:27

♪PINO♪
Cute compared with Nicoletta, I suppose
18:27

ONIKO
Ehhh, cute compared with Nicoletta
18:27

NICOLETTA
What am I to you all?
18:28

✿MAKO✿
Perv
18:28

♪PINO♪
Dunce
18:28

ONIKO
Masochist
18:28

NICOLETTA
Praise me more
18:28

HERO
Those aren't compliments
Read 18:28

NICOLETTA
I should warn you.
There's nothing cute
about Cass 18:35

HERO
Huh? She looks beautiful
to me
Read 18:36

NICOLETTA
No, I don't mean it in that
sense. Hmm, how should I
put this...? 18:36

MAKO
Isn't she really good with the
internet? 18:36

NICOLETTA
Yeah, she's poor at combat,
so she spends all her time on
her PC 18:36

NICOLETTA
She runs some kind
of website where she
rounds up content from
around the internet. I
think she calls it a blog? 18:37

HERO
Whoa, that's amazing. I feel
like we'd really get along

What kind of content is on the
website?
Read 18:37

NICOLETTA
I actually don't know
much about it 18:38

ONIKO
I've seen it once 18:38

ONIKO
There was a really long
feature presenting info on
Nicoletta's sexual fetishes 18:38

HERO
Wut...?
Read 18:38

HERO
I'm interested in meeting her
Read 18:42

NICOLETTA
Oh really? 18:42

NICOLETTA
You seem to have piqued her
curiosity as well, Hero 18:42

HERO
Wow, I'm flattered
I might try reaching out to
her over SNS
Read 18:43

MAKO
Hero...
You should stop
now 18:43

HERO
Huh, why?
Read 18:43

PINO
It's exactly like I said

Cass is fine...compared with
Nicoletta 18:43

ONIKO
Hmm, is there a word to
describe kids like her? 18:43

MAKO
"Very
affectionate"
would be one
way to put it 18:43

HERO
Isn't that a good thing?
Read 18:44

NICOLETTA
I gave her your contact info,
so she may reach out to you 18:44

HERO
Ok
Read 18:44

CASS

Helloooooooooooooooooooooooooooo
ooooooooooooooooooooooooooooooo
ooooooooooooooooooooooooooooooo
ooooooooooooooooooooooooooooooo
ooooooooooooooooooooooooooooooo
ooooooooooooooooooooooooooooooo
ooooooooooooooooooooooooooooooo
ooooooooooooooooooooooooooooooo
ooooooooooooooooooooooooooooooo
ooooooooooooooooooooooooooooooo
ooooooooooooooooooooooooooooooo
ooooooooooooooooooooooooooooooo
ooooooooooooooooooooooooooooooo
ooooooooooooooooooooooooooooooo
ooooooooooooooooooooooooooooooo
ooooooooooooooooooooooooooooooo
ooooooooooooooooooooooooooooooo
ooooooooooooooooooooooooooooooo
ooooooooooooooooooooooooooooooo
ooooooooooooooooooooooooooooooo
ooooooooooooooooooooooooooooooo
ooooooooooo Hero! I'm Nicoletta's
little sister, Cass, nice to meet you
haha, I heard you're traveling with
my beloved sibling and to be totally
honest I feel nothing but hate,
loathing, anger, and resentment
toward you for tying her down, but
she told me not to bother you, so I'll
refrain from killing you, but Hero,
no, "Hero" doesn't feel right, maybe
I'll call you big bro, not that I have
any real reason to call you that, but
if you're traveling with my sis then
that kinda makes you my big bro
and having an older brother would
make me happy and open my mind
up to new fantasies and stuff which
sounds really fun, though a
manservant is never allowed to
touch my sis even if she's a masochist,
she's mine, and you're my obedient
manservant, and don't you forget it.
Also, sorry to change the subject,
but I've never talked to a boy before
because my personality is this way,
but Sis has been telling me to be
more social (I guess?), anyway this
is pretty much a first for me, so
sorry if I say anything weird... Lolol.
Did you believe that apology there's
no way I'd care what some guy I've
never met thinks, I'm a VAMPIRE for
crying out loud, humans are nothing
but food for us, and you should go
ahead and offer your blood to me,
what kind of blood do you

CASS

Hey Hero, why haven't you been
responding to my messages I
wonder if I said something to weird
you out? Answer meeeeeeeeeeeeee
eeeeeeeeeeeeeeeeeeeeeeeeeeeeeee
eeeeeeeeeeeeeeeeeeeeeeeeeeeeeee
eeeeeeeeeeeeeeeeeeeeeeeeeeeeeee
eeeeeeeeeeeeeeeeeeeeeeeeeeeeeee
eeeeeeeeeeeeeeeeeeeeeeeeeeeeeee
eeeeeeeeeeeeeeeeeeeeeeeeeeeeeee
eeeeeeeeeeeeeeeeeeeeeeeeeeeeeee
eeeeeeeeeeeeeeeeeeeeeeeeeeeeeee
eeeeeeeeeeeeeeeeeeeeeeeeeeeeeee
eeeeeeeeeeeeeeeeeeeeeeeeeeeeeee
eeeeeeeeeeeeeeeeeeeeeeeeeeeeeee
eeeeeeeeeeeeeeeeeeeeeeeeeeeeeee
eeeeeeeeeeeeeeeeeeeeeeeeeeeeeee
why do you talk to other girls and
not me, you're mine, you know, your
head, your body, your ears, your
face, your heart, your blood, your
nails, your everything all belongs
to me, I guess I could let you talk
to Nicoletta a little, but if you chat
with other girls I won't forgive you
I'll tear you down on my website
in a public, humiliating fashion I'll
have it all over the internet that
you're a pervert lolol so Hero how
would you describe your love for
me? Ah, sorry, I shouldn't ask you
things like that out of the blue. I
wonder if that was annoying, but
you don't mind, right, cause I know
you love me more than anything
in the whole wide world, I'll let
you marry me, even though I'm
a shut-in and I don't have much
confidence in myself I know you'll
love me forever big bro and I love
you second most after my sis so
you don't have to worry, you'll let
me wrap you up like a mummy
and suck your blood right? Oh,
but if you're the type that likes to
feel pain and stuff, let me know
ASAP, I'll do whatever makes you
happiest lolol, you might not have
expected this, but you'll be glad
to hear I'm actually pretty good at
household chores, I don't really like
laundry and cooking and cleaning
and stuff, but I'm sure I could learn,
so yeah, I'm definitely going to
make a good wife. Why aren't you
responding to me big bro? Are you
with another girl or

CASS
Answer meeeeeeeeeeeeeeeee eeeeeeeeeeeeeeeeeeeeeeeeee eeeeeeeeeeeeeeeeeeeeeeeeee eeeeeeeeeeeeeeeeeeeeeeeeee big brooooooooooooooooooooo ooooooooooooooooooooooooo ooooooooooooooooooooooooo ooooooooooooooooooooooooo ooooooooooooooooooooooooo let me suck your blooooooooo ooooooooooooooooooooooooo ooooooooooooooooooooooooo ooooooooooooooooooooooooo ooooooooooooooooooooooooo oooooooooooooooooooooooood I know yours will be delicious and if I had it, I wouldn't need anything else at all, though I do want my sis to be here because I'm lonely. I wonder when you're going to come visit me, it's funny, I've never seen you once, and yet my chest is pounding, and I think extracting ▓▓▓▓▓▓▓▓▓ ▓▓▓▓▓▓▓▓▓ from your ▓▓▓▓▓▓▓▓ licking up the ▓▓▓▓▓▓▓▓▓▓ ▓▓▓▓▓▓▓ like an ice cream would be pure bliss big bro big bro big brooooooooooooooooo ooooooooooooooooooooooooo ooooooooooooooooooooooooo ooooooooooooooooooooooooo ooooooooooooooooooooooooo ooooooooooooooooooooooooo ooooooooooooooooooooooooo ooooooooooooooooooooooooo why won't you answer me? I'm sure you're being seduced by some other girl big bro big bro big bro big bro I want to know more about you big bro big bro big bro big bro big bro I hate being apart from you, and I want you to respond big bro big bro big bro big bro big bro big bro big bro respond to me big bro big bro big bro big bro I'll kill you if you don't respond I'll kill you big bro big bro big bro you promised you'd let me suck your blood big bro why don't you answer? I'm going to keep messaging you until you

 CASS
Hey big bro, why won't you respond to me? You've clearly seen my messages, you know how much I'm thinking of you, you need to reciprocate my feelings, and remember that your everything belongs to me big brooooooooooooooo ooooooooooooooo you're mine big bro you're mine I don't understand why you won't respond

Whyyyyyyyyyyyyyyyyyyyyyyy yyyyyyyyyyyyyyyyyyyyyyyyyy yyyyyyyyyyyyyyyyyyyyyyyyyy yyyyyyyyyyyyyyyyyy answer meeeeeeeeeeeeeeeeeeeeeeeee eeeeeeeeeeeeeeeeeeeeeeeeee eeee I'll suck ALL your blood all your blood I'll suck suck suck suck you like me don't you? You like me don't you? Don't yooooooooooooooouuuuu uuuuuuuuuuuuuuuuuuuuuuuuuu uuuuuuuuuuuuuuuuuuuuuuuuuu uuuuuuuuuuuuuuuuuuuuuuuuuu uuuuuuuuuuuuuuuuuuuuuuuuuu uuuuuuuuuuuuuuuuuuuuuuuuuu uuuuuuuuuuuuuuuuuuuuuuuuuu uuuuuuuuuuuuuuuuuuuuuuuuuu uuuuuuuuuuuuuuuuuuuuuuuuuu uuuuuuuuuuuuuuuuuuuuuuuuuu uuuuuuuuuuuuuuuuuuuuuuuuuu uuuuuuuuuuuuuuuuuuuuuuuuuu uuuuuuuuuuuuuuuuuuuuuuuuuu uuuuuuuuuuuuuuuuuuuuuuuuuu uuuuuuuuuuuuuuuuuuuuuuuuuu uuuuuuuuuuuuuuuuuuuuuuuuuu

 CASS
I'm gonna get some ice cream 21:32

Read 21:33 **HERO** ...That sounds nice

 [somebody help]

Once upon a time, in a certain corner of the world, a young couple lived with their child in happiness.

"See you later!" the five-year-old called out energetically. Despite the early hour, he left the house with little more than a practice sword and a small shield. His dream was to become a renowned hero who fought for the people, just like his father was.

"Oh, that boy always forgets his lunch," his mother remarked with a smile and a sigh after discovering the food she'd made was still sitting on the table.

"It'll be fine. I'm sure he'll come back once he's hungry," his father said before folding his newspaper and finishing off his morning soup.

"Okay, I'm going to go gather some firewood from the mountain so our brave son doesn't catch a cold."

"Good idea. I'll go do the laundry at the river so you two have no lack of clean clothes to wear."

After saying lines straight out of some old, familiar tale, the couple also ventured off.

By the way, these parents had a heating unit in their house, so they didn't have a particular need for a fireplace or fuel. They also had a washing machine that ran using magic power, but it seemed that the mother still preferred to use fresh water from the river now and then. The exact reason for this remained unknown.

"Yahhh! Haaah!"

The boy set right to swinging his sword in the forest that he had made his training ground. Only weak monsters with low intelligence appeared there, so there were none he couldn't fend off on his own.

He became so immersed in his practice that he lost track of time. Before he knew it, night had arrived.

"All right, that feels like a good place to stop for today."

He spoke with a level of intelligence one would never have expected from a five-year-old. He then refilled his canteen at a lake and leaned back against a tree to rest.

"I want to become an even greater champion than Dad so that I can protect this beautiful world," stated the boy, staring up at the star-filled sky. Once again, this proclamation displayed a surprising level of comprehension for a young child.

"Huh...?"

That was when it happened. Something appeared in the sky that looked less like a shooting star and more like a bright mass of energy. As though on cue, it began to descend as soon as the boy took notice of it. The object crashed near a big tree in the forest.

"D-did something just fall?!"

The boy bolted to the impact site, moving as if drawn to it. At his age, it was difficult for him to contain his curiosity, and his legs hurried to carry him to the tree.

"Is that…a person?!"

Although still a few dozen paces away, the young child spotted the unmistakable shape of a person. The foliage around them had been burned, likely from the explosive crash. Undoubtedly, this person was what had fallen. However…

"They're surrounded!"

A pack of wolf monsters had emerged from the forest, happy for easy prey. Weakly, the person in the crater opened their eyes. Upon realizing their predicament, their face went pale.

"I need to save them!!"

The boy gripped his practice sword and charged heroically at the monsters.

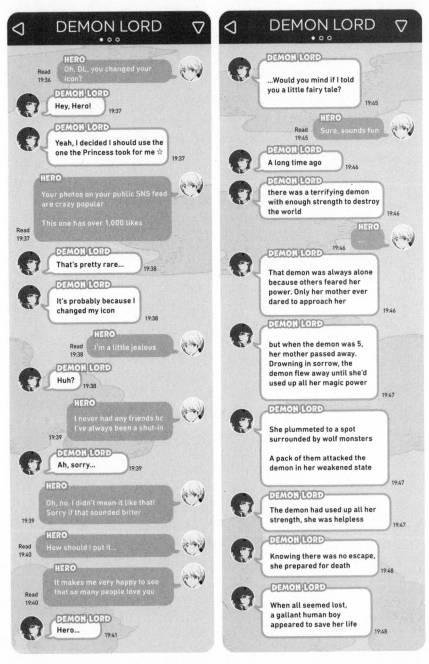

IF THE RPG WORLD HAD SOCIAL MEDIA...

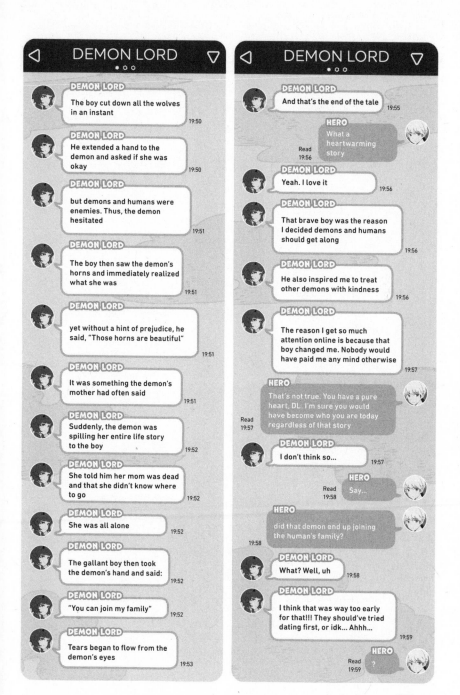

HERO
Read
14:50
Hey, I can see the next town

HERO
Read
14:51
Wait, what are those 5 huge towers around it?

PINO
The tombs of the legendary Six Sages who sleep in Nextland
14:51

HERO
Read
14:51
...Six Sages?

NICOLETTA
How is it possible for a human to have not heard of the Six Sages...?
14:52

PINO
They fought a Demon Lord 300 years ago
14:52

HERO
Read
14:52
Ah, I've probably seen that on the internet before. Does that mean they fought the Demon Lord's grandfather?

MAKO
Maybe her great-great-grandfather
14:52

PINO
Demons usually despise humans, but even we recognize the greatness of the Six Sages
14:53

HERO
Read
14:53
Why's that?

ONIKO
Cause the Demon Lord at the time tried to wipe every man from existence except for himself to create his own Harem Kingdom
14:53

HERO
Read
14:54
Asshole

PINO
"I'm gonna be the Harem King!!!"

That was his catchphrase
14:58

HERO
Read
14:59
I'll say it again

Asshole

ONIKO
Male demons obviously hated his guts
14:59

HERO
Read
14:59
...Wait a second, 5 tombstones for 6 sages?

NICOLETTA
One was a masochist who ghosted the rest for attention
14:59

NICOLETTA
That's my guess   14:59

HERO
Read
15:00
Yeah, right

MAKO
I don't know for sure, but I think one left on some kind of journey
15:00

HERO
Read
15:00
Just like a certain legendary Hero

PINO
The Six Sages were initially revered heroes called the "Ira Sutoya"

It's an undeniable truth that they saved the world
15:01

PINO
Let's visit their tombs once we're in town
15:01

WONN
...I feel an evil energy 16:30

WONN
The time for revival is nigh

Fellow Six Sages, let us awake from our long slumber 16:31

TEW
...Oh-ho, four evil souls of considerable strength 16:31

THRIE
But their power does not approach ours. Unfitting sacrifices 16:32

WONN
Fear not. Sicks has already found an offering fitting for our return 16:32

FORE
Yes, I can sense it. There's a sinister energy far to the west 16:32

FYVE
Haha, what welcome news. I assume Sicks is there already 16:32

TEW
But we lack vitality and mobility under our graves. How are we to lure it into the Magic Pentagram? 16:32

WONN
There is no need for concern. Sicks has been sending me regular updates in our personal chat. Everything is moving according to plan 16:33

DEMON LORD
Princess, where are you? 17:55

DEMON LORD
It's almost evening

That's enough hide-and-seek 17:55

PRINCESS
Read 17:56
Oh, that's too bad...

PRINCESS
I was hiding in your bed stark naked

Read 17:56
I wish you had found me...

DEMON LORD
I see

Don't catch a cold 17:56

DEMON LORD
Hey, Nanny, I'm getting kinda hungry 17:56

DEMON LORD
Can you start dinner? 17:57

NANNY
Understood 17:57

NANNY
My lord 17:57

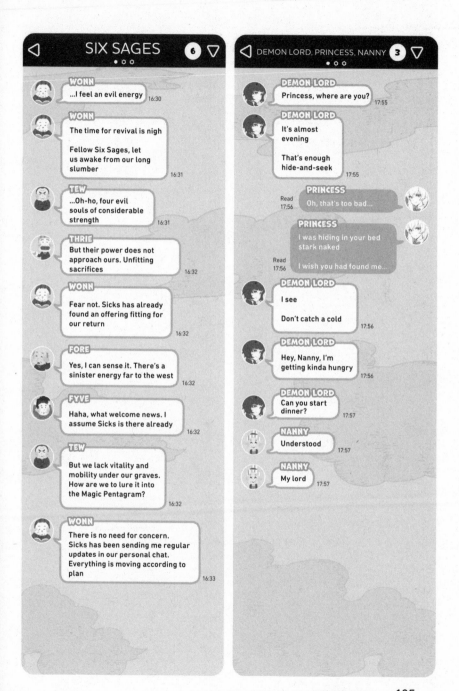

HERO
Read 19:25 — Man, that was a hassle

HERO
Read 19:25 — but I did finally get them to change before we entered the town...

DEMON LORD
Haha. That sounds rough 19:26

DEMON LORD
Nice job, Hero 19:26

HERO
Read 19:26 — Uh, thanks

HERO
Read 19:26 — I've had a lot to deal with, but this is probably the most fun I've had in my entire life

DEMON LORD
Really? 19:26

HERO
Read 19:26 — Yeah

HERO
Read 19:26 — I have a goal. I have friends

It's nice

DEMON LORD
...It makes me happy to hear you call the Demon Generals friends 19:27

DEMON LORD
And what's that goal? 19:27

HERO
Read 19:27 — ?

HERO
Read 19:27 — To see you, obviously

DEMON LORD
D 19:28

DEMON LORD
Don't startle me! No fair!!! 19:28

NANNY
Ms. Pino 21:30

NANNY
I hope you are doing well. This is Nanny 21:30

♪PINO♪
Read 21:31 — Hello, Nanny

♪PINO♪
Read 21:31 — We made it to the town of Balse

NANNY
Well done
Thank you again for the favor 21:31

♪PINO♪
Read 21:31 — It's nothing. I would never refuse a request of yours

♪PINO♪
Read 21:32 — The Demon Lord's birthday is in 2 days. I'll bring you a bottle of Deepsleep Whiskey, as I promised

NANNY
I'm so sorry for the trouble
I'm very grateful you would entertain an old lady's request 21:32

♪PINO♪
Read 21:33 — I'm only returning the favor for all the years you have been by my master's side

NANNY
That fills me with joy to hear 21:33

NANNY
Let's make her 17th birthday a grand celebration 21:33

♪PINO♪
Read 21:33 — That sounds great. The DG will return to the castle in 2 days for the party

NANNY
I look forward to it 21:33

YUSUKE NITTA 137

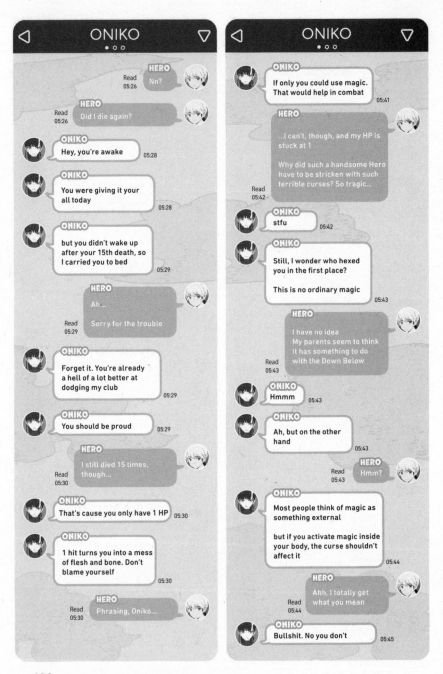

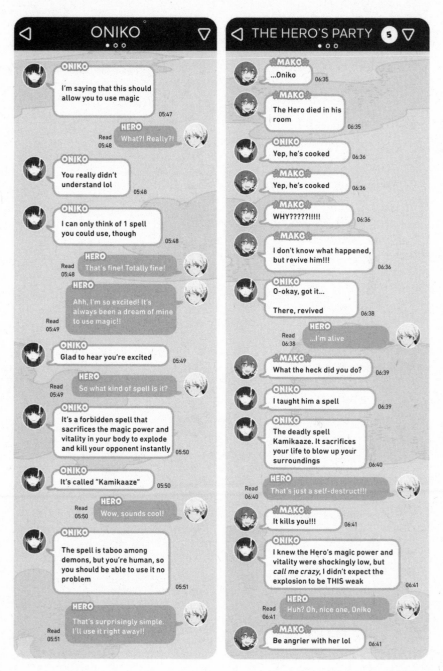

ONIKO
I'm saying that this should allow you to use magic
05:47

HERO
Read 05:48
What?! Really?!

ONIKO
You really didn't understand lol
05:48

ONIKO
I can only think of 1 spell you could use, though
05:48

HERO
Read 05:48
That's fine! Totally fine!

HERO
Read 05:49
Ahh, I'm so excited! It's always been a dream of mine to use magic!!

ONIKO
Glad to hear you're excited
05:49

HERO
Read 05:49
So what kind of spell is it?

ONIKO
It's a forbidden spell that sacrifices the magic power and vitality in your body to explode and kill your opponent instantly
05:50

ONIKO
It's called "Kamikaaze"
05:50

HERO
Read 05:50
Wow, sounds cool!

ONIKO
The spell is taboo among demons, but you're human, so you should be able to use it no problem
05:51

HERO
Read 05:51
That's surprisingly simple. I'll use it right away!!

MAKO
...Oniko
06:35

MAKO
The Hero died in his room
06:35

ONIKO
Yep, he's cooked
06:36

MAKO
Yep, he's cooked
06:36

MAKO
WHY?????!!!!!
06:36

MAKO
I don't know what happened, but revive him!!!
06:36

ONIKO
O-okay, got it...
There, revived
06:38

HERO
Read 06:38
...I'm alive

MAKO
What the heck did you do?
06:39

ONIKO
I taught him a spell
06:39

ONIKO
The deadly spell Kamikaaze. It sacrifices your life to blow up your surroundings
06:40

HERO
Read 06:40
That's just a self-destruct!!!

MAKO
It kills you!!!
06:41

ONIKO
I knew the Hero's magic power and vitality were shockingly low, but *call me crazy*, I didn't expect the explosion to be THIS weak
06:41

HERO
Read 06:41
Huh? Oh, nice one, Oniko

MAKO
Be angrier with her lol
06:41

YUSUKE NITTA   139

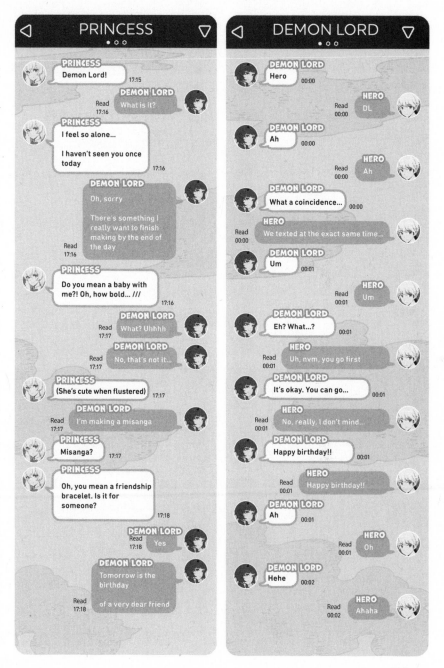

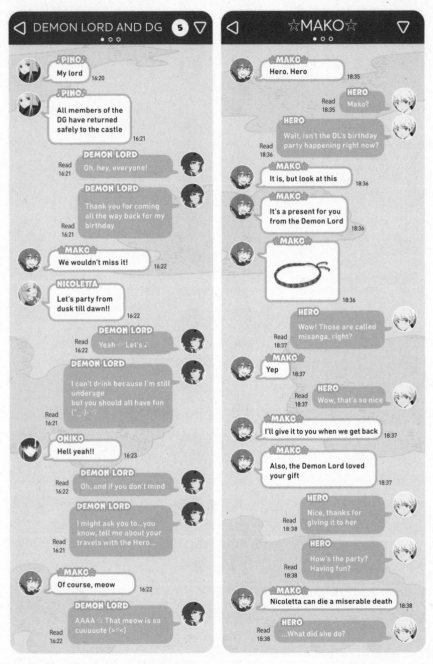

♪PINO♪
My lord
16:20

♪PINO♪
All members of the DG have returned safely to the castle
16:21

Read 16:21
DEMON LORD
Oh, hey, everyone!

DEMON LORD
Thank you for coming all the way back for my birthday
Read 16:21

MAKO
We wouldn't miss it!
16:22

NICOLETTA
Let's party from dusk till dawn!!
16:22

Read 16:22
DEMON LORD
Yeah ♪ Let's ♪

DEMON LORD
I can't drink because I'm still underage
but you should all have fun (´_-)-☆
Read 16:21

ONIKO
Hell yeah!!
16:23

Read 16:22
DEMON LORD
Oh, and if you don't mind

DEMON LORD
I might ask you to...you know, tell me about your travels with the Hero...
Read 16:21

MAKO
Of course, meow
16:22

Read 16:22
DEMON LORD
AAAA ☆ That meow is so cuuuuute (>♡<)

MAKO
Hero. Hero
18:35

Read 18:35
HERO
Mako?

HERO
Wait, isn't the DL's birthday party happening right now?
Read 18:36

MAKO
It is, but look at this
18:36

MAKO
It's a present for you from the Demon Lord
18:36

MAKO
18:36

Read 18:37
HERO
Wow! Those are called misanga, right?

MAKO
Yep
18:37

Read 18:37
HERO
Wow, that's so nice

MAKO
I'll give it to you when we get back
18:37

MAKO
Also, the Demon Lord loved your gift
18:37

HERO
Nice, thanks for giving it to her
Read 18:38

HERO
How's the party? Having fun?
Read 18:38

MAKO
Nicoletta can die a miserable death
18:38

Read 18:38
HERO
...What did she do?

NICOLETTA
Whoo-hoo-hoo-hoo-hoo
Whoo-hoo-hoo-hoo-hoo
19:11

HERO
Read 19:12
Um...?

NICOLETTA
The Demon Lord hates me...
19:12

NICOLETTA
Whoo-hoo-hoo-hoo-hoo
Whoo-hoo-hoo-hoo-hoo
19:12

HERO
Read 19:13
Is that supposed to be crying? Lol

MAKO
She asked the Demon Lord to step on her...
19:13

NICOLETTA
It looked like she really wanted to do it!!!!
19:13

PIINO
don'td worrry Piino, the demon lord doesn' hate you thaaaaaaat mcuh
19:13

ONIKO
Not at allllll!!!!
19:13

HERO
Lolwut
I'm guessing they're all drunk
Read 19:14

MAKO
Everyone's drinking except me
19:14

HERO
Read 19:14
Why aren't you?

MAKO
I'm not good with alcohol (-_-;)
19:15

MAKO
Nanny, the Demon Lord's aide, provided drinks for us
19:19

MAKO
so I guess I should have a little
19:19

HERO
Read 19:20
Well, make sure to take it easy

HERO
Read 19:20
I didn't know the Demon Lord had an aide

MAKO
Nanny has served the Demon Lord for a long time
19:20

MAKO
The Demon Lord lost her mother at a young age
19:21

MAKO
So Nanny is like a mother to her meoooooooooooooooo ooooooooooooooooooooooo oooooo
19:21

HERO
19:21
Huh?

HERO
19:22
What happened?

HERO
19:22
Wait, it doesn't say you've read these. Are you already drunk?

HERO
19:22
Eh, whatever

HERO
19:23
I guess I'll enjoy my own birthday party alooooooooooooooo

HERO
19:39
Sorry, some soldiers captu

When the Demon Lord returned to the party from the bathroom, there was an uproar.

The Demon Lord, who was wearing a gorgeous jet-black dress, was the star of the celebration, but the five hundred or so female demons in attendance were all afraid that they would be incinerated if they didn't maintain magical barriers when in her presence.

"…"

A hint of gloom crept into the Demon Lord's expression. She used to emit power strong enough to disintegrate anyone in her vicinity until she was five, but thanks to eight years in the Holy Spring, she no longer possessed that dreadful ability.

It was even safe for her to interact with humans now. Her time spent with the Princess, a powerless young woman, was proof enough of that.

Sadly, old impressions and rumors didn't die easily. Some looked on in envy at the Demon Lord's beauty and strength, but most kept their distance.

Many of the demons attended the party simply to score some points with the greatest of their kind. Whether it was asking for poverty relief or wanting permission to maintain control of old captured human territory, they always came to her with their problems and petitions.

Naturally, the Demon Lord understood what they were trying to do, and she knew that the great majority of the "likes" that she got on social media were also just given to get on her good side.

"...Hey, Princess."

The Demon Lord spotted the beautiful (on the outside) girl whom she had accidentally abducted from LMAO Castle. The Princess looked exceedingly noble in the brand-new, custom-made dress that the Demon Lord had ordered for her. Despite her graceful appearance, she was hurriedly tasting and comparing the hundreds of cakes that had been prepared for the event.

"Oh, Demon Lord! H-h-h-h-how do you do?" the Princess said upon spotting her.

"How are the cakes? I heard that Nanny carefully selected the very best from among those that are popular in human society," the Demon Lord stated with a smile.

"They're all absurdly delicious! I can't believe that food this good is truly real! My father is always trying to save money, so I could never have imagined this level of extravagance back at my castle!"

The Princess could not stop stuffing herself, even with her beloved Demon Lord right in front of her.

The Demon Lord didn't see the behavior as rude. Instead, she found it endearing. Obviously, the Princess harbored an uncommon level of affection for her, which made things slightly uncomfortable. Still, the Demon Lord appreciated that the Princess expressed her true feelings rather than hiding them. There was no deceit.

The Demon Lord didn't trust the Princess over the Demon Generals, of course, but she was grateful for her openness. It was a world away from the female demons who smiled to the Demon Lord's face while whispering things like "Make sure to keep your distance from the Demon Lord" and "Don't forget your shield" behind her back.

"I'm glad you like them. Enjoy the party to the fullest, Princess. I asked Nanny to make your bed for you. If you get tired or have too much to drink, you can rest in your room."

"What?! Aren't we sleeping in the same bed tonight?!"

"...I don't remember promising anything like that..."

"Are you kidding me?! You said you would, Dilly!"

"Who is Dilly?"

The Demon Lord skillfully dodged the Princess's advances and began walking back to her seat.

"Demon Lord! Good day to you. I am the vice commander of the Dullahan Tribe. I am honored to celebrate your birth on this most inauspicious of days, for you are both the heavens and evil incarnate—"

"Demon Lord, what a lovely day this is. I am the wife of the leader of the Troll Tribe. You recently rejected my husband's proposed invasion of a human settlement over SNS—"

"Demon Lord, I—I—I am the l-l-leader of the s-s-skeletons. I h-h-heard that you want p-p-peace with the humans. As a f-f-former human in life, I am g-g-greatly moved—"

"Hey, can't you all see you're bothering the Demon Lord? You should be ashamed of your greed. Ah, pardon the interruption, Demon Lord. I am Mino, a secretary for Minotaur Group LLC. We have a contract we would love you to take a look at—"

One demon representative after another foisted their request upon the Demon Lord, competing for her attention with various forms of flattery.

This was easy to forget given the cease-fire established three years prior, but there were some among these demons whose diet had consisted primarily of humans, and others who had kept them as slaves. Such activities had been their livelihood, but now they couldn't even invade human land without permission from the Demon Lord.

Many demons had lost their families to human warriors and pleaded with the Demon Lord for revenge.

The Demon Lord didn't intend to make light of their petitions, but she ensured that none of her people would harm humans.

However, there were those sly negotiators who sidled up with contracts designed to swindle money from the Demon Lord's estate. The young woman was inexperienced in such matters, so she left the negotiations to her trusted aides.

"Hey, listen up! The Demon Lord is clearly exhausted, so that is enough for tonight."

Head in her hands, the Demon Lord looked up when Nanny, an aide who had served her family for over one hundred years, arrived to rescue her.

"Nanny!" The Demon Lord was so relieved to see her face. She quickly scurried to hide behind the old woman.

"Can't you see the toll this is taking on her? There is no way she can discuss matters with a clear head when crowded in such a fashion. Now get away! Scram!" Nanny exclaimed, quickly waving her hands to drive back the throngs of demons.

None knew if Nanny had the power to back up such a command, but her status as a direct attendant to the Demon Lord left few willing to push their luck.

"Sorry that you had to do that for me, Nanny."

"Don't worry about it. I can handle fools like them in my sleep. I have no family of my own, and I owe the Demon Lord family for graciously taking me in. You're like a granddaughter to me, my lord."

"Thank you."

The Demon Lord sighed, and she scanned the venue for someone she could talk to without reserve… Unfortunately, there was no such person in attendance. Her trusted members of the Demon Generals—Mako, Nicoletta, Pino, and Oniko—were nowhere to be seen.

"…Huh? Nanny, do you know where the Demon Generals went?"

"Ah, yes. They are all currently indisposed, likely from overindulgence of alcohol. I carried them to their beds while you were in the bathroom."

"Really? Thank you, Nanny."

"It was nothing, child. I only did what is expected of me. I am sure they were tired from their journey with the Hero as well."

"Huh, but…" A single doubt rose in the Demon Lord's mind. "Mako doesn't drink. Did she pass out, too?"

"…Yes. She was undoubtedly overjoyed to see you again after so long apart. I'm afraid she collapsed almost immediately. She doesn't handle her liquor well, it seems."

It didn't make sense to the Demon Lord that Mako would drink in her presence. After all, the beastman was bad with alcohol. Still, she couldn't imagine that Nanny would lie.

"…I see."

"Okay, it is almost time to end this party. I'm sure you're tired, so I will handle the closing remarks. You go on to bed, dear."

"Yeah, I'll do that. Thank you, Nanny."

The two exchanged a smile and walked side by side. Any strangers who saw them would have mistaken the pair for a grandmother and granddaughter.

No sooner had the Demon Lord returned to her room than she flopped on the bed.

She may have brought this on herself by driving out her father, the Demon Overlord, but she was fed up with parties. They made for good opportunities to improve relations between demons and humans, but talking to so many people was exhausting.

"Haaah…"

The Demon Lord buried her head in the sheets and sighed.

How wonderful would it be if she had a person who loved her by her side at times like these? The visage of a certain boy appeared in the back of her mind.

They had never met. Well, technically, they *had* seen each other once. Plus, in the social-media era, you could see what someone looked like even if you had never met them via their profile picture. The icon didn't tell her everything about him, but she was still grateful that she could see his face despite the distance between them.

"Hero…," the Demon Lord muttered to herself. She then rolled onto her back and lifted her smartphone. She checked her messages, but there was nothing from the Hero.

She felt a sudden wave of emotion and tapped his icon to enlarge it. A relaxed smile spread across her lips.

Thoughts of what he was doing began to drift about her mind. He was likely relaxing after enjoying dinner in Balse. It then occurred to the Demon Lord that he wouldn't be training with Oniko that night, so she tapped on their text thread and sent him a message.

[What are you doing right now?]

It felt unlikely that he'd respond immediately, but the Demon Lord's heart still pounded as she waited for the notification that he'd read her text. One, two, five minutes passed, yet he still hadn't checked it.

He's been sleeping outside his entire journey, so he's probably taking this chance to enjoy a good night's rest in a soft bed, the Demon Lord reasoned.

"Ah..."

Her eyes caught the strap dangling from her phone—a birthday present from the Hero. Two little wooden people dangled from a thin thread. The Demon Lord had attached the gift to her smartphone as soon as she'd received it from Mako, but things had been too busy during the banquet to examine it.

One of the figures looked like a sweet girl with horns on her head, and the other was a brave boy holding a sword. When the Demon Lord looked closely at the girl, she could tell that the Hero had glued on the horns himself.

"Ha-ha..."

Smiling, the Demon Lord tapped the trinket. This caused the girl to peck the boy on the cheek, and the Demon Lord blushed a deep shade of red.

If only days like this could last forever..., the Demon Lord thought as she calmly drifted off to sleep.

Late at night, when all the attendees had left the castle and all the maids were asleep, someone slinked down the corridors of the palace, holding a candle.

Her body was hunched. She struck her hip with one hand and let out a sigh, then made a thin, creepy smile that suggested some plot of hers was progressing exactly according to plan.

"All capable of standing in our way will be extirpated," she muttered. The crone opened a hidden door somewhere in the wall of the passage, which led to a chamber where four demons were sleeping comfortably on the floor. It was Mako, Nicoletta, Pino, and Oniko, the members of the Demon Army's Four Demon Generals.

"As I am now, I cannot kill you. But I can manage this."

The old woman set her candle on a desk in the hidden room and began to chant a spell under her breath. The window in the secret chamber then blew open, and she screamed, "*Kazoomkle!*"

Four times, she intoned the spell, and with each incantation, a member of the Demon Generals was enveloped by luminous particles and hurled out the window. Unlike the teleportation spell Zoomkle, which sent you to a specified location, Kazoomkle flung the target to a totally random, faraway place.

"...The Demon Generals have been broken and scattered...and the Deepsleep Whiskey will have them out for a while yet...," the old woman said with glee, though slightly out of breath. Kazoomkle wasn't incredibly advanced magic and didn't require much power to use, but casting it four times in a row had to be a lot for one her age.

"It's almost time... Nyeh-nyeh-nyeh, now, if I can just get ahold of that body..."

Wind blew in softly from the window, causing the flame of the candle to illuminate her face. The light revealed none other than the aide who served the Demon Lord family for hundreds of years, the woman whom the Demon Lord thought of as a mother-like figure—Nanny. A sinister grin rested on her face.

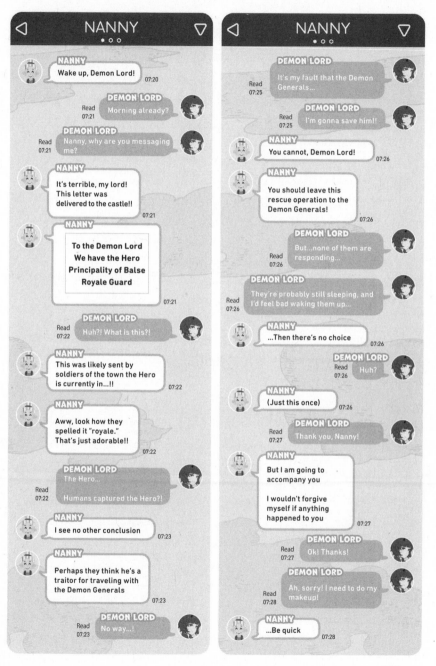

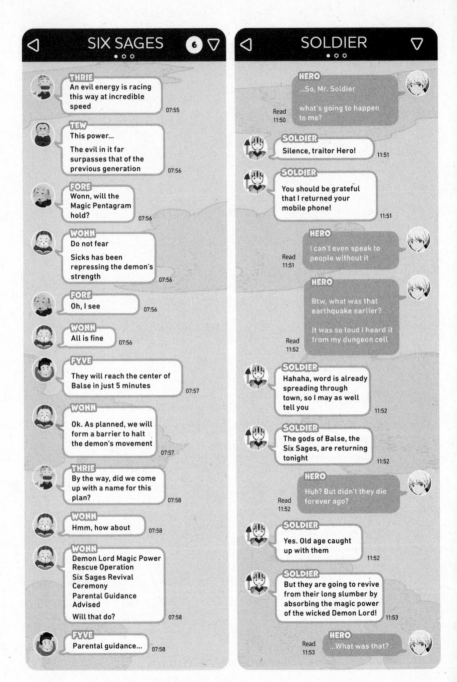

THRIE
An evil energy is racing this way at incredible speed
07:55

TEW
This power...
The evil in it far surpasses that of the previous generation
07:56

FORE
Wonn, will the Magic Pentagram hold?
07:56

WONN
Do not fear
Sicks has been repressing the demon's strength
07:56

FORE
Oh, I see
07:56

WONN
All is fine
07:56

FYVE
They will reach the center of Balse in just 5 minutes
07:57

WONN
Ok. As planned, we will form a barrier to halt the demon's movement
07:57

THRIE
By the way, did we come up with a name for this plan?
07:58

WONN
Hmm, how about
07:58

WONN
Demon Lord Magic Power Rescue Operation Six Sages Revival Ceremony Parental Guidance Advised
Will that do?
07:58

FYVE
Parental guidance...
07:58

HERO
...So, Mr. Soldier
what's going to happen to me?
Read 11:50

SOLDIER
Silence, traitor Hero!
11:51

SOLDIER
You should be grateful that I returned your mobile phone!
11:51

HERO
I can't even speak to people without it
Read 11:51

HERO
Btw, what was that earthquake earlier?
It was so loud I heard it from my dungeon cell
Read 11:52

SOLDIER
Hahaha, word is already spreading through town, so I may as well tell you
11:52

SOLDIER
The gods of Balse, the Six Sages, are returning tonight
11:52

HERO
Huh? But didn't they die forever ago?
Read 11:52

SOLDIER
Yes. Old age caught up with them
11:52

SOLDIER
But they are going to revive from their long slumber by absorbing the magic power of the wicked Demon Lord!
11:53

HERO
...What was that?
Read 11:53

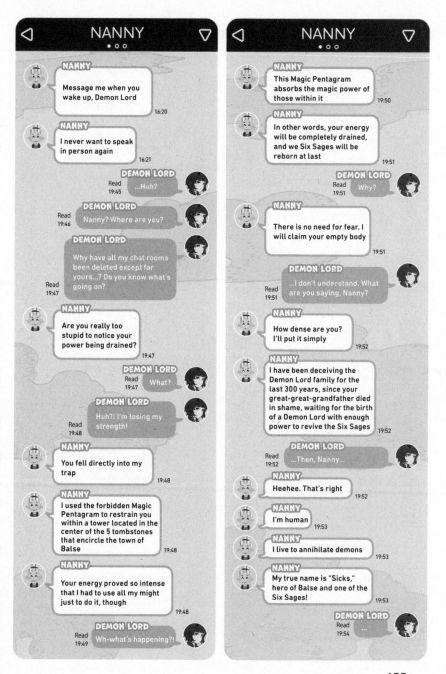

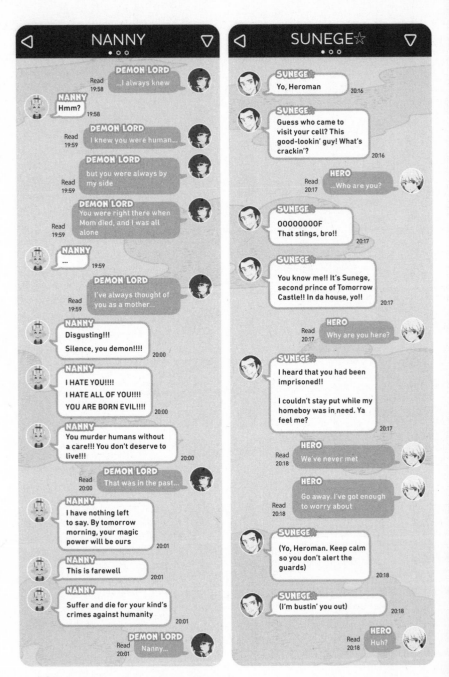

MAKO
Then Nanny...! — 21:05

NICOLETTA
Betrayed us?! — 21:05

PINO
...I'm sorry — 21:06

PINO
She played me for a fool. I led the Hero to Balse and left him there alone — 21:06

PINO
I even bought the whiskey she used to put us to sleep... — 21:06

PINO
Nanny sent me a message saying "Hahaha, I tricked you, you dimwit demon!" — 21:06

ONIKO
That old hag!!! — 21:07

NICOLETTA
I'm gonna kill her!! — 21:07

MAKO
Wait, let's calm down. She likely wants us to lose our cool — 21:07

MAKO
Where are the Demon Lord and the Hero? — 21:07

PINO
I received a message saying the Demon Lord is having her magic power drained in the Balse Central Tower — 21:07

PINO
As for the Hero... Idk. Captured probably — 21:08

ONIKO
We have to save them!! — 21:08

NICOLETTA
Yes, I sure do love pain — 21:08

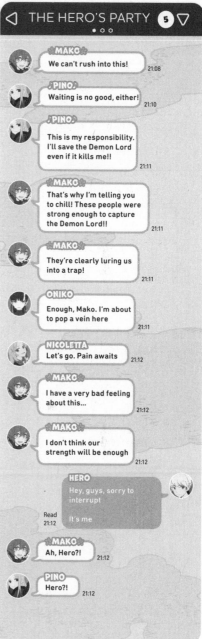

MAKO
We can't rush into this! — 21:08

PINO
Waiting is no good, either! — 21:10

PINO
This is my responsibility. I'll save the Demon Lord even if it kills me!! — 21:11

MAKO
That's why I'm telling you to chill! These people were strong enough to capture the Demon Lord!! — 21:11

MAKO
They're clearly luring us into a trap! — 21:11

ONIKO
Enough, Mako. I'm about to pop a vein here — 21:11

NICOLETTA
Let's go. Pain awaits — 21:12

MAKO
I have a very bad feeling about this... — 21:12

MAKO
I don't think our strength will be enough — 21:12

HERO
Hey, guys, sorry to interrupt
Read 21:12
It's me

MAKO
Ah, Hero?! — 21:12

PINO
Hero?! — 21:12

YUSUKE NITTA   157

NICOLETTA
Hero! You're safe!! 21:13

MAKO
Thank goodness 21:13

HERO
Sorry, everyone

They used me as a hostage to lure in the Demon Lord
Read 21:13

PINO
No, it was my... 21:13

ONIKO
We can blame ourselves later 21:13

ONIKO
I'm gonna kill the shitheads who took the Demon Lord 21:14

HERO
Hey, let's just calm down
Read 21:14

HERO
We're facing the legendary Six Sages

We're unlikely to win unless we stay levelheaded
Read 21:14

NICOLETTA
You know what exists between calm and passion? Pain!!! 21:15

HERO
Quiet, you
Read 21:15

MAKO
Hero, are you really okay? 21:15

MAKO
How did you escape capture? 21:15

HERO
I'll tell you later lol
Read 21:15

HERO
Ok, first, let's gather at the oasis near Balse. We can plan out a course of action there
Read 21:16

ONIKO
Got it, I'll go there with Zoomkle 21:16

HERO
Let's meet in an hour
Read 21:16

HERO
I'll do some research into the Six Sages in the meantime
Read 21:16

MAKO
So they're really going to be resurrected? 21:17

HERO
...Yeah. Seems so
Read 21:17

HERO
We'll have to fight them to save the Demon Lord
Read 21:17

ONIKO
Hey, what do you mean by "research"? 21:17

HERO
We live in an era where everything is online. There has to be some strategy or weakness out there
Read 21:18

PINO
There's no way this will be that easy! You can't possibly know which articles on the internet are even the slightest bit trustworthy!! 21:18

HERO
I know someone who can help us with that...
Read 21:18

NICOLETTA
Hmm? 21:18

HERO
She's a bit difficult, but she knows everything on the internet
Read 21:18

The Hero looked up at the sky as he raced through the pitch-dark desert. It was cold enough for him to see his breath.

It was his fault that the Demon Lord had been captured. That wasn't going to be easy to forget, though this was hardly the time for wallowing.

"Always choose to look ahead over dwelling on regrets. If you fail, then think of the best way to fix it and keep moving forward." Something the Hero's father had once said to him surfaced in his mind.

Papatega wasn't the best father, but the Hero did look up to him to an extent, and the man was a former hero in his own right. Perhaps that saying was one passed down through the Hero's family for many generations. It could even carry some mysterious power. While unlikely, the Hero decided that this was true.

The girl he was reaching out to would probably kill him once he saved the Demon Lord. But after telling himself that such a fate would (hopefully) be nothing compared with Oniko's training, the Hero messaged Nicoletta's little sister, Cass.

[Hey, Cass, how's it going? Sorry to bother you, but I've got a request.]

[Wow, bold of you to ask me for something after ignoring, like, *all* my messages, you know where you stand, right, you must get how I feel sending you messages all this time, so first of all, I'm going to have to demand nine liters of blood as an apology. Do you know what that means? Lolol. An adult human male only has about four and a half liters of blood, so you'll be offering me, like, two people's worth of blood as a compulsory tribute, but it's the right thing to do if you think about it, although, even if you gave it to me, I wouldn't be allowed to drink it because that Demon Lord girl has outlawed all vampires from drinking human blood, so you'll be breaking her rules, but as long as you're okay with that...]

Her message continued like this for a while.

The Hero had known what he was getting into when he had texted her.

If her words alone are this overpowering, what in the world is she like in real life...? The Hero paled at the mere thought. While they were communicating over the internet, he read every word so as not to be impolite. When Cass's messages finally slowed, he quickly explained his reason for reaching out to her.

[...Wow, that sounds fun.] In a break from her usually obsessive behavior, Cass got on board surprisingly quick. Maybe she was glad to have someone ask her for help for the first time in her life.

Cass's socialization had always been very one-sided. She wound up running a popular blog somewhat accidentally through the simple process of posting about her hobbies and her sister's sexual fetishes. Never had someone come to her asking for a favor.

Like the Hero, she was a shut-in, so he could guess what kind of personality she had and what she would want in return.

[I'll get back to you with text files after I gather enough info. This won't take long!]

Unlike her in previous messages, Cass's sentences were now short and only conveyed what was necessary.

It turned out that being a shut-in did have its advantages. Cass was a good writer, she was proficient at getting things done quickly, and she worked with precision because she was experienced with locating and uploading accurate data. The risk of online backlash had honed her into the sort who meticulously verified their stories before posting them.

"Okay..."

A small wave of relief washed over the Hero when he received the fruits of Cass's efforts.

"...This is gonna work!"

The Hero immediately checked through each document, and every time he responded, Cass would get back to gathering more intel about the Six Sages and the town of Balse.

Unfortunately, Cass was a little too quick at her work. In every free moment, she would continue to bombard the Hero with incredibly long stalker-style messages.

♪PINO♪
I'm at the oasis
22:18

ONIKO
I see the Hero
22:18

☆MAKO☆
...He looks kinda exhausted
22:19

HERO
You don't know what I've been subjected to in the last hour...
Read 22:19

NICOLETTA
Cass...
22:19

♪PINO♪
What about the plan?!!
22:19

HERO
I think it'll work
Read 22:19

HERO
The Six Sages are currently in their tombs around Balse. The graves are positioned in the shape of a pentagram, and underneath each one, the Six Sages are all absorbing the Demon Lord's magic power
Read 22:19

HERO
The problem is the Demon Lord isn't in any of them. She is on the top floor of the Balse Central Tower
Read 22:20

☆MAKO☆
?
2:20

☆MAKO☆
Wouldn't that mean all we have to do is reach the top floor of the tower and save her?
22:20

HERO
No, it won't be that easy
Read 22:20

HERO
A really annoying barrier has been put on the spire. Only those permitted by the Six Sages can pass through
Read 22:21

♪PINO♪
So, we just have to dispel the shield
22:22

HERO
Logically, yes
Read 22:23

HERO
This is what makes that forbidden Magic Pentagram spell so annoying, though
Read 22:23

HERO
The barrier is set up so that it can't be removed as long as it is connected to at least one of the Six Sages
Read 22:23

♪PINO♪
I don't get it!! Explain simpler!
22:23

HERO
Basically, we need to fight each of the 5 sages underneath the tombs simultaneously
Read 22:23

HERO
If we do that, their connection will be interrupted and the barrier will temporarily fade
Read 22:23

HERO
but the Six Sages are gaining strength, and most would die for them immediately
Read 22:23

HERO
I asked Cass to estimate their present power
Read 22:24

HERO
To put it bluntly, they are so strong that not even Mako could win in a one-on-one fight, and she's the best fighter we've got
Read 22:24

NICOLETTA
Seriously?!
22:24

ONIKO
Even she's mad
22:24

HERO
Read 22:25
It's okay

HERO
Read 22:25
I already know their weaknesses, and I have countermeasures

NICOLETTA
Nice
22:25

☆MAKO☆
So we gotta fight each of the sages solo?
22:26

HERO
Read 22:26
Simply put, yes

☆MAKO☆
Imma smash em
22:26

♪PINO♪
But we're one short. There are 5 tombs and 5 sages, excluding Nanny. What about the last one?
22:27

NICOLETTA
The Hero will handle it. He's a masochist, remember?
22:27

HERO
Read 22:27
I'm not
and I'd die lol

HERO
Read 22:28
About the last one. I actually have a request from someone...but we're gonna need Pino's help

♪PINO♪
Huh? Me?
22:28

HERO
Read 22:28
Yep. This person said they'd listen to any request you give them

♪PINO♪
That's weird
22:29

♪PINO♪
So, who is this person?
22:30

♪PINO♪
It doesn't seem likely they'll be able to stand against one of the Six Sages, whoever they are
22:30

HERO
Read 22:31
Don't worry about that Those brothers are a strong combo

♪PINO♪
Brothers? All right. I'll ask them
22:31

HERO
Read 22:31
...You know how I said he'd do anything, right?

HERO
Read 22:32
Ok, here he is

♪PINO♪
?
22:32

The Hero invited Hamige to the group.
Hamige joined the group.

HAMIGE
MY SWEET, LOVELY PINO!!!
22:33

HAMIGE
I'm here. There's no need to fear. I'll do anything you ask! I'd walk on hot coals for you!!!
22:34

HAMIGE
You need my help... If that's true, then it's no stretch to say we're lovers, nay, husband and wife!
22:34

☆MAKO☆
omgroflmao
22:34

NICOLETTA
Hamige? Lolololol
22:34

♪PINO♪
I'll kill you, Herooo!!!!
22:34

YUSUKE NITTA   163

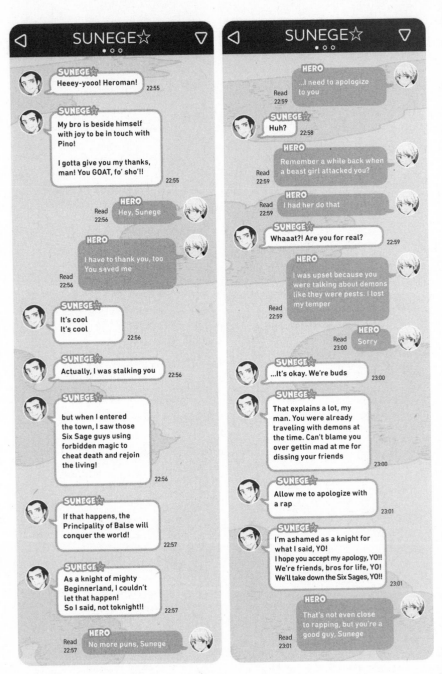

☆MAKO☆
Hero, let's hear your plan
23:05

HERO
Read 23:06
Ok

HERO
The Six Sages are easy to keep straight because they're named after numbers
Read 23:06

HERO
Wonn, Tew, Thrie, Fore, Fyve, and Sicks

Those are the people we'll be fighting
Read 23:06

NICOLETTA
Who's taking who?
23:06

HERO
Uhhh

HERO
Read 23:06
It'll be faster to show you this

HERO
Sage [Wonn] vs Mako
Stronger than the others
Weakness is arthritis in right shoulder

Sage [Tew] vs Oniko
Weakness is revival magic, surprisingly

Sage [Thrie] vs Pino
Strong up close but bad against ranged magic

Sage [Fore] vs Nicoletta
Strong against magic but mentally weak

Sage [Fyve] vs Hamige bros
Weakest sage but need to watch for insta-kill magic

Sage [Sicks] vs Hero
I'll fight her once the barrier is dispelled
Read 23:06

ONIKO
Okay, simple enough
23:07

NICOLETTA
Nice handwriting, Hero. Lol
23:07

HERO
Read 23:07
Piss off

☆MAKO☆
This "Wonn" is the strongest?
23:08

HERO
Yeah, sorry, Mako. We have no choice but to leave him to you
Read 23:08

☆MAKO☆
It's fine. I'll manage somehow
23:08

♪PINO♪
All right!! Plan set!! What are we waiting for?!!
23:09

HERO
Read 23:09
Uh, Pino? Lol

ONIKO
She's probably desperate to get away from Hamige
23:09

HERO
Read 23:09
Ah. Lol

NICOLETTA
We don't have until tomorrow morning. Let's go
23:09

HERO
Read 23:09
Sorry. Hold up a sec

☆MAKO☆
What?
23:10

HERO
I know I've taken charge of this situation, but I can't stop shaking
Read 23:10

NICOLETTA
Are you okay, Hero?
23:10

HERO
Honestly, no. Give me a minute

HERO
Read 23:11
I've gotta find some courage

YUSUKE NITTA   165

I was always alone.
Always in solitude.

The Demon Lord was only three years old when she first felt that way. It was around then that her power first began to show itself, and the things she touched began to decay and melt.

She was still a young child, so she found it fun and started touching anything that captured her interest. One day, however, she poked a sturdy, steel-made toy and watched it crumble. Unable to understand what had happened, she started crying and threw herself at her mother, who was still alive at the time.

"There, there. I know that was scary. But you're okay now. See, you can touch Mommy and Daddy. We're not going to melt."

Every time the Demon Lord sobbed, her mother would soothe her by patting her on the head and gently talking her down. None understood the Demon Lord the way her mother did.

Despite her fears, the Demon Lord's power grew steadily greater. Eventually, the ground beneath her began to melt, and those with low magic power feared that merely standing in her presence would destroy them.

An official notice was then issued to every demons to keep a healthy distance from the Demon Lord under all circumstances. She was forbidden from interacting with anyone other than her parents or her aide, Nanny. Any who saw her approaching in the castle turned and fled.

When the Demon Lord was five, her mother died of illness.

Officially, the story was that the woman had been terminally ill. However, the Demon Lord was old enough to wonder if she had been the real cause of her parent's condition.

Young though she was, her power already eclipsed her father's, and even he started vomiting blood when he touched her. From then on, the Demon Lord was denied physical contact with her family, and she fell into total isolation.

The days that followed were spent alone.

The Demon Lord had to keep her distance from her mother's bed when she watched the woman. Despite the risk, however, her mother mustered the last of her strength to call her daughter toward her. She then hugged her and said, "I love you, Demon Lord... I know there is—"

The Demon Lord could only barely hear her mother over her own sobs. After expressing her undying love, the Demon Lord's mother departed this world.

...Mom, why did you die...?

...Was it because of my terrible power...?

...It was my fault...
...I killed Mom...

It didn't take long for the Demon Lord to reach this conclusion.
"Wahhhhhhhhhh!!!"
While wailing, she unleashed an explosion of magic power and took off flying from the Demon Lord Castle.

The Demon Overlord pursued her immediately, but the five-year-old was already the strongest creature on the planet, and he had no chance of catching her. If any humans had happened to glance up at the right time, all they would've seen was a distant object hurtling through the sky faster than a shooting star.

Mom died because of me.
Other demons are suffering because of me.
Humans despise me.
What should I do?
Mom is gone.
I make things hard on Dad.
...Being alive is too painful.

Everyone hates me...
The world would be better off...
...if I didn't exist.

Hopeless, the Demon Lord flew until she exhausted her magic power, the life source of demonkind, and crashed into a big tree in some unknown land.
I should just die.

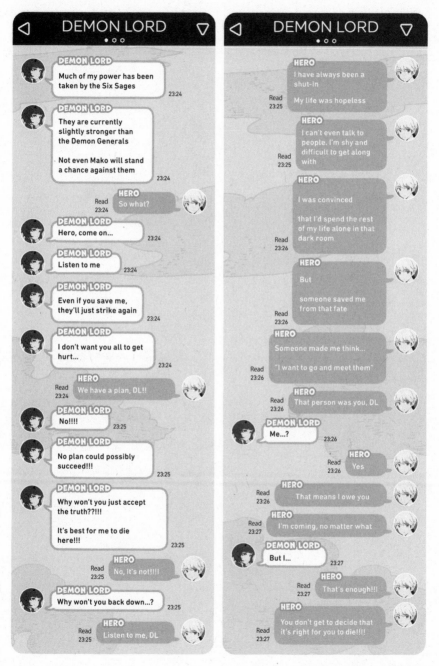

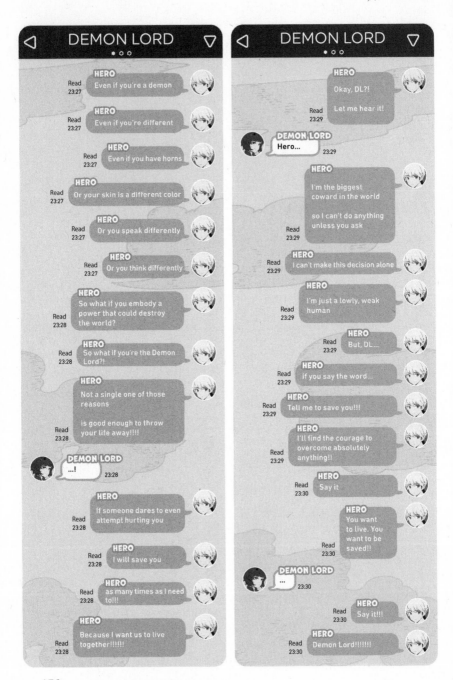

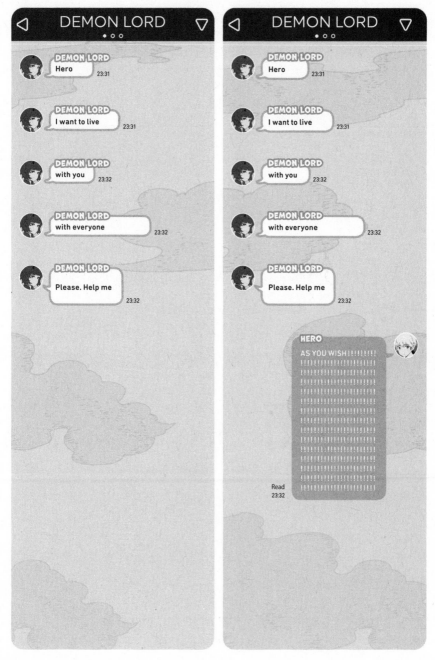

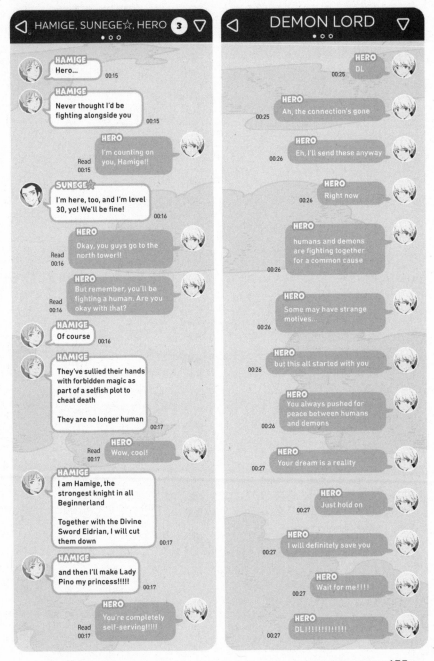

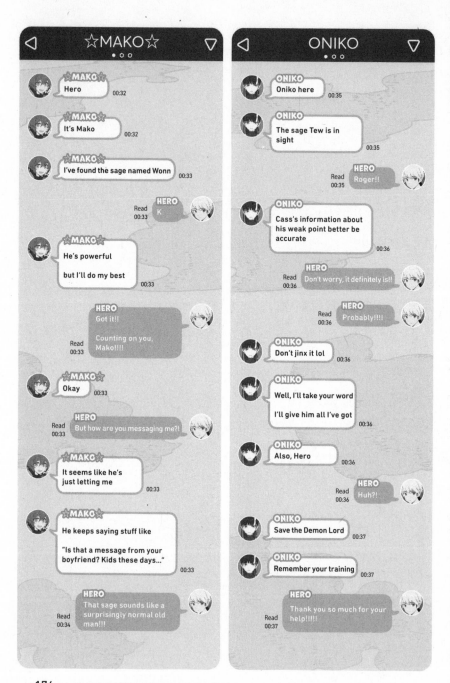

IF THE RPG WORLD HAD SOCIAL MEDIA...

The Principality of Balse rested in the middle of the desert, surrounded by a permanent cloud of sand.

Rain was rare. No one would argue that living in such a place was easy, but the king had built his nation there for two reasons. The first was the defense that the harsh environment provided against invaders. The second was to ensure that the remains of the legendary humans known as the "Ira Sutoya" could rest in peace deep below the earth.

These champions were a party of six people who had been assembled to put a stop to a previous Demon Lord's destructive whims. They eventually triumphed and enjoyed great praise for it.

Unfortunately, this sextet was also filled with maniacs who refused to accept death.

A *hero* was one who possessed a strong sense of justice and couldn't turn a blind eye to people in need. They were the sort who'd risk it all to help others. The six entombed below Balse were not regarded as *heroes* but rather *sages*, and that was not without reason.

Not one of them was a kind person, nor did any possess a strong conscience. They'd only challenged the Demon Lord to flaunt their strength.

It was rumored that before their climactic struggle against the embodiment of evil, the Six Sages had all been deviants who enjoyed toying with humans and demons alike.

They carried out merciless experiments on the demons they captured, seeking to find the most painful methods of death. By sapping souls and strength from others, they extended their own life spans. At times, they'd even resort to stealing bodies.

The Six Sages were not ordinary people. They were just as twisted by insanity as the Demon Lord of their era, and that was what had enabled them to oppose him.

There was no denying they were infinitely strong. They were also shrewd strategists.

After they fought the Demon Lord, they formed a plan to rest their injured bodies for hundreds of years and then recover their youth by using someone with extremely strong and terrible magic power. They sealed themselves away in a safe location and hypnotized generations of Balse kings into building a suitable environment for their scheme.

As a result, the tombs constructed for the Six Sages underneath the town of Balse were vast and tough. Astoundingly, the catacombs were larger than the castle town above. Iron and stone encased the structures, blocking out all light.

The expansive desert terrain of the Balse region enabled the tombs to be arranged in the shape of a pentagon, and the Six Sages had also constructed a solid prison to ensure their safety for when it came time to absorb the impossibly strong magic power of someone like the current Demon Lord.

"...Okay."

After she finished messaging the Hero, Mako flicked the smartphone in her right hand into the air with her thumb. The object soared above her messy red hair and floated there. Its liquid-crystal display captured Wonn performing his warm-up exercises.

Wonn had the elderly body of a human man in his late seventies. However, his glossy skin and the black aura flowing from his form were proof enough that he had already absorbed some of the Demon Lord's power.

"I'm not the type to enjoy hitting girls, little missy," Wonn admitted suddenly in a near whisper. Mako twitched, unable to hide her anger.

"...How *gentlemanly* of you. Naturally, that means it's okay for you to absorb magic power from the Demon Lord, who happens to be a girl, right?" Mako spat.

Her smartphone landed cleanly into her pocket, and she folded her arms and glared threateningly at Wonn.

"Don't be ridiculous. The Demon Lord is a cretin that must be eliminated—regardless of gender. That *thing* cannot be called a girl. It is a repulsive creature that plunges the world into fear. It is a malign god of destruction that steals countless lives."

A crease formed on the brow of Mako's usually sweet face. "...This is actually a relief, you know. You being this much of a piece of trash is going to make this easier, *meow*."

The beastman demon stretched her neck and glowered at Wonn as if she were looking at a worm. She then concentrated her animalistic instincts and dropped into a crouch to release the overwhelming force in her legs. Mako was the fastest member of the Demon Generals, and all that strength was currently leveled at this old man who had dared to cross her master.

"Hoh-hoh. A lowly beast could never hope to stop me as I am now."

Wonn, who was considered the mightiest among the Ira Sutoya Six Sages, waved his hands and assumed a martial-arts stance—that of a style that aimed to suppress the opponent's power.

The ominous ebon vapor flowing from his body collected around his hands and feet. His honed combat senses made it extremely easy for him to master the vast magic power he had absorbed from the Demon Lord already.

Just like the guy said, he is definitely stronger than me "as he is now." He has experience fighting a previous Demon Lord on equal footing, and he's leeching the Demon Lord's magic power. If my strength as the strongest of the Demon Generals is a seventy, his strength is a one hundred, meow.

Mako's body burned with anger, but her mind was cool. She could tell instantly from her opponent's flawless guard alone that he was stronger than any human she had ever encountered.

Thankfully, his drooping right shoulder suggested that the tip about his arthritis had been correct.

"Good job, Hero... All that's left now is to kill him," muttered Mako.

The great strength in Mako's feline legs continued to build until it caused the muscles in them to swell to double their size. With this, Mako was able to charge at the speed of sound—a feat that had earned her a reputation as the fastest individual in the entire Demon Army.

"Hoh-hoh, I'm impressed."

Wonn could sense his foe's strength and seemed to guess that holding back would not be an option.

"We probably won't be able to talk as we fight, so I'll go ahead and speak my mind now. You all lured the Demon Lord into a trap by taking advantage of her pure heart and kindness. You betrayed her wish to improve relations between demons and humans... For that reason, I'm going to kill you," Mako stated.

"...Then allow me this reply. I can't imagine a more absurd notion than unity with wickedness given form. And a beast like you should know better than to defy a human," Wonn answered.

A second later, the two combatants disappeared. Cracks began to form on the walls of the tomb. It was a fight too fast for normal eyes.

Shortly after Mako and Wonn began their clash, Oniko was staring fixedly at the sage named Tew in the southeast tomb.

"...Call yourself a Six Sage or whatever the fuck else you like, but you're just a bigoted old man," Oniko snarled, lifting her club and resting it on her shoulder. Tew was small of stature, only reaching four feet tall, but he was floating in the air to meet his enemy's eyes.

"You have an unthinkably dirty mouth for a girl. That's a reflection of your poor upbringing," Tew fired back in a mocking tone.

Like Wonn, he had also siphoned power from the Demon Lord, and dark energy radiated from his body. As the atmosphere of the room grew increasingly strained, both settled into their combat stances.

The Hero told me that revival magic is effective against this guy, but why? I could just try using Relife repeatedly, but he's clearly stronger than me. I need to avoid running out of magic power until I figure out why revival spells would hurt him.

Despite her foul mouth and massive weapon, Oniko was the sort who preferred to think things through.

Her role in battle was to heal the party, similar to a priest. However, if she ran out of MP, which were the magic points that enabled one to use spells, she became the kind of club-wielding muscle-brain you'd expect a lot of demons to be.

Oniko had made it into the Demon Generals because of her huge MP supply and talent for recovery magic. She was also quite skilled with teleportation spells.

"Hey, ogre, are you just going to stand there? Not that someone of your level of strength would stand a chance against an immortal like me," Tew jeered.

"...Huh? Immortal?"

"Did you not wonder how the Six Sages, who perished three hundred years ago, still manage to walk the realm of the living? ...Well, you'll understand soon enough."

After that ominous statement, Tew's left arm suddenly separated from his body and plopped to the ground. It was as if he had cut it off himself.

"God, that's disgusting! What the hell was that?!"

"If that surprised you, just wait for what comes next."

The severed limb steadily grew in size, eventually forming into a second Tew. It didn't just look like him; by cutting off a part of his body, he'd created a second self just as authentic as the original.

And he didn't stop there. Tew lopped off his right arm, his legs, and even his limbless torso from under his neck. Before long, there were five copies for a total of six Tews. The original sprouted a new little body as though it were the most natural thing in the world.

"After sacrificing many lives during long years of experimentation, this is the strongest magic I managed to create. They may be products of fission, but they are all just as capable as I am. You know what that means, right? You have to fight six of me at once, each of us possessing the strength of one of the Six Sages."

Evidently, Tew was quite proud of himself, as he and his duplicates all grinned eerily at the original's pompous monologue.

"...It is seriously creepy watching six of the same face smile at the same time," Oniko said with an expression of disgust. She spit on the ground in evidence of that. "I should have known all you Six Sages were off your rocker. I don't give a damn about the lives you've already sacrificed, but whether they be demon or human, none of them will be able to rest in peace after dying for your stupid research. I pity their souls."

"What are you saying? My subjects offered themselves to me. For me and the prosperity of this world."

"Ha, are you saying the Demon Lord offered her magic power to you of her own volition? If so, then you're just delusional. I doubt any of them were willing, which would mean you forced them all to participate."

Irritated, Oniko swung her club through the air with her right hand, then pointed her left hand at Tew in a threatening pose.

"...Quit your yappin' already and come at me. Talkin' to you makes me want to puke. I'm gonna kill all six of you!"

The Tews eyed her blankly, then smirked in unison.

"Give me all you've got," they muttered before charging at Oniko.

Meanwhile, Pino was fighting Thrie in the northwest tomb. She kept her distance and prepared to use offensive magic, her specialty, by spreading her black wings wide in flight and gathering magic power in the air.

This wasn't to suggest that she possessed low amounts of magic power. It was simply because her opponent had proven to be a foe skilled enough to restrain the Demon Lord. She couldn't risk anything but her best against such an enemy.

"Hoh-hoh, you seem quite skilled," Thrie praised with ample confidence as he watched Pino soar through the sky. It was clear he wasn't taking her seriously. His body was old, but possibly due to the energy he had absorbed from the Demon Lord, he had straightened up his spine.

"You're an angel, aren't you? I heard a rumor once that some kind of heavenly tribe lives way up above the clouds. Ah, but you have black wings. Are you perhaps a fallen angel, driven out from the heavens?"

"Silence."

Pino didn't have the slightest bit of intention of talking to the sage. Unsurprisingly, much of that was because she wished to save the Demon Lord as quickly as possible, but she also feared that Thrie would discover her strategy if they continued to banter. According to the Hero's intel, Thrie excelled in melee combat. Pino wanted to control the pace of the battle as best she could and avoid getting too close.

"What terrible manners you have. I just woke up for the first time in three centuries. I would've liked a bit of decent conversation, even if you are a demon."

"..."

Although Pino knew there was no need to feel sympathy for this old man, her inner kindness distracted her for a brief moment.

"Where'd he go?!"

That was all Thrie had needed to disappear. Losing sight of him for even a split second risked disaster. Pino quickly scanned her surroundings, afraid he had fled.

He had not.

"I'm right here."

A thud reverberated through the room as a sharp pain ran up Pino's back. With speed and strength that was far beyond what any regular person could achieve, Thrie had circled quickly behind Pino and delivered a heavy kick.

"Tch!"

Pino clicked her tongue and stopped herself in the air just before she collided with the wall. If she hadn't been aware of her opponent's proficiencies, that move would have knocked her out. Thankfully, she had used a spell to bolster her defense before the fight.

"Impressive. You're slender but quite tough," remarked Thrie.

Pino maintained her posture in the air and used a recovery spell to mend her injury. Thrie watched her with an expression of ease. His blow proved there was a significant difference in their level of strength.

"He's a monster…"

The sage significantly surpassed Pino in almost every way. Realizing this, Pino had no choice but to keep her distance and rely on what she was good at: magic. She concentrated the power she had collected from the atmosphere around her hands, shot a powerful fire spell at Thrie, then worked another bit of magic to increase her strength.

"Whoa! That's some impressive spellcasting you've got there." Despite the compliment, Thrie evaded the flames handily. "I see this could get dangerous if I don't take this seriously."

"You and your foolish Six Sages will fall here for what you've done to the Demon Lord," declared Pino.

Wasting no time, she hurled ice and wind magic at him, moving back to increase the distance between them every time she did so. Thrie was swift, and Pino blocked him with physical reflect and counterspells whenever he charged at her. The man seemed to be overjoyed at the prospect of his first strong adversary in years. Even when Pino landed a direct hit on him, he would laugh loudly and keep coming.

"Mwa-ha-ha-ha-ha! This is great, fallen angel! Let's have some fun!"

"...You're a simpleton who only thinks of brawling. I'll burn you to a crisp!"

Having now each confirmed the other's abilities, they charged at the other with full strength, unconcerned about the walls crumbling around them.

Nicoletta had realized something the moment she stepped foot inside the tomb of the one named Fore.

"This room..."

It was starkly empty. While it was the same shape as the chambers the other members of the Demon Generals were fighting in, Nicoletta felt there was an essential element missing.

"Where are the candles, whips, and blades? Why do I not see any weapons? Are the Six Sages not professionals of torture?! No matter how far I walk, it's just walls, walls, and more walls! What in these empty rooms could possibly satisfy me?!"

That's right. That absent necessity was pain.

Agony ruled supreme for Nicoletta, to the point that it could even be called her purpose for living. But there was nothing in the tomb that could satisfy her.

Suddenly, she hit upon an idea.

"I'll crash into the wall!!"

How she arrived at that notion was a little difficult to understand, but the vampire intended to sate her desires by whatever means necessary. Yet in a curious bit of irony, her wish for pain was granted.

"You're pretty annoying, you know."

A kindly voice speaking insulting words echoed through the chamber and was immediately followed by a powerful blow to Nicoletta's back. Fore, who had concealed himself in the dark, caught Nicoletta completely unawares and struck her with a powerful uppercut. Before she even knew what was happening, she smashed hard against the wall.

"Hey, what the heck?!!" Nicoletta screamed, not even fazed. Turning as she slid down the wall, she leveled a finger at Fore. "That attack was too fast for me to process! Unfair!"

A small amount of blood dripped from her mouth when she stood up.

"…That's because it was a surprise attack," Fore responded.

"What a waste!!!" bellowed Nicoletta. Fore stared at her in confusion, unable to comprehend what this crazy girl was so upset over.

"From now on, when you attack me, do it properly. If the attack comes too swiftly, I have no time to savor the agony. That is an unforgivable insult to pain."

Fore could not figure out why Nicoletta was upset but eventually decided she was simply off in the head.

"Well, now I know you're an absolute lunatic. Sorry about before," he said.

"Very good. Be careful next time," responded Nicoletta.

A strange atmosphere had formed between the two. Undoubtedly, it would have been too weird for any observer.

"You appear to be a vampire, but is it safe for me to assume you are an assassin in service to the Demon Lord from whom we are currently absorbing magic power?"

"That's right. But there's one more thing you should know. I am an extreme masochist. Please abuse me to your heart's content."

Fore stared at Nicoletta with his mouth agape. After a moment, he elected not to ponder on that unnecessary information for too long.

"But the Demon Lord is not a masochist," Nicoletta appended meekly. "She welcomed me with an open mind, without judging me for who I am. Other people always looked the other way and ignored me completely, but she allowed me to serve her. It had to have been embarrassing for her to choose me as a member of the Demon Generals. Do you see what I'm getting at? The Demon Lord is the nicest, greatest, and purest person in the world. All she wants is peace. For an outcast like me, she is my one shining beacon of hope."

It was rare to see Nicoletta so serious. Her reasoning made sense.

"For that reason, pain does not suit the Demon Lord, and she does not wish for it, either. You're forcing it on her for greedy designs—reasons that lack excess sadism or masochism, and are barren of love. What you've done is an arrogant act of self-pleasure."

"...H-huh."

How long is she going to go on? thought Fore.

"You tricked the Demon Lord and inflicted her with the greatest possible *mental* pain. In exchange, you will give me, Nicoletta, the weakest member of the Demon Generals, the greatest possible *physical* pain."

Fore was still having a hard time getting a sense of what exactly she wanted to say, but now that it seemed like she was done talking, he could finally get a word in.

"...Uhhh, if that's what you want, then I'll attack you now. Is that okay?"

"There's no need to hold back. Come at me with all you've got!!"

"You got it."

Fore bent down into a crouch and dashed toward Nicoletta with a sonic boom. He punched, kicked, chopped, kneed, elbowed, head-butted, and hit her with every kind of physical and magical attack one could think of.

...Huh?

As Fore beat Nicoletta to a pulp, something felt off to her.

"Gah, blargh, ahh, oof..."

She couldn't even speak through the onslaught of attacks. Every strike landed accurately on a vital point, and her HP was being steadily chipped away.

"No, wai—"

"What's the matter? You told me to give you everything I had."

Fore then hit her with a finishing move square in the chest, causing a comic-book-esque *pow* to echo throughout the tomb and sending Nicoletta crashing against the wall a second time.

"Gahh!!"

Yet again, she'd received the much-desired wall collision, but after she fell to the ground, she noticed something odd within herself.

This is weird.

Nicoletta felt different today. This pain should have felt good, but instead, her body was rejecting it and crying out.

"It can't be..."

A moment later, Nicoletta heard the violent roar of an empty stomach.

I see. Now that I think of it, I haven't sucked human blood in many years. I was satisfied during my last withdrawal episode by a full-on bombardment of adorableness, but this sage is showing me no mercy.

A vampire can only go so long without blood. I didn't think I'd reach my limit here, but my hunger has numbed my cranial nerves that convert pain to pleasure.

I can't let myself just die like this. If I perish, then the Six Sages' barrier won't dispel, and we'll lose our chance at saving the Demon Lord.

The Demon Lord allowed me to serve her even though I'm a masochist and everyone thinks I'm a freak. I can't betray her. I want to save her, and not because she could give me more incredible pain than anyone else in the world.

I want to save the Demon Lord because...she accepted me.

It's definitely not because she showers me with greater agony than anyone in the world. That's so important that I have to repeat it. That is certainly not the reason.

For the sake of the Demon Lord, I can't afford to lose.

"Nrgh..."

Nicoletta's consciousness was fading. In a last-ditch effort for help, she threw away her pride and began to message a certain boy.

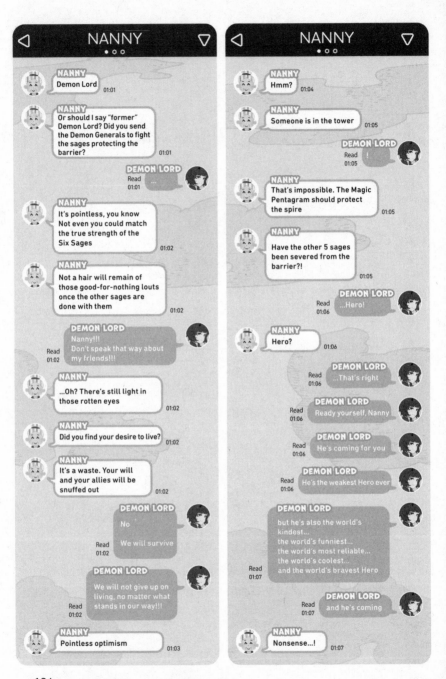

IF THE RPG WORLD HAD SOCIAL MEDIA...

An impact shook the tomb to the southwest of Balse like never before. Pieces of the impossibly strong walls crumbled, kicking up clouds of dust.

The cause of the tremor was an extremely high-speed object entering the tomb for the second time.

"Wh-what's happening?!"

Fore, who had been fighting Nicoletta until just a moment ago, couldn't so much as guess at this new development. The vampire had disappeared just moments after he thought he'd killed her, and then the whole place shook a few minutes later.

"I'm baaaaack!"

Things soon became clear, however. Nicoletta had returned, looking fresh-faced. She gave a smile and a wink.

"H-how is this possible?! My last move should have killed you!" Fore screamed, a cold sweat breaking out on his face. Something about this felt even more ominous and repulsive than when he'd fought a Demon Lord, and goose bumps formed on his whole body.

"Sorry about before. That was an embarrassment to all masochists everywhere."

The woman's eyes were bloodshot, and some kind of powerful, purple miasma was gushing out of her body. It seemed a task all unto its own for her to maintain control in her ecstatic state.

"But now I'm back to my usual self! All right, Fore. Hit me with everything you have! I feel aroused in the greatest, strongest, most wonderful way! Punch me, kick me, suck me, cut me, stab me, hurl me, abuse me! Give me pain! WRYYYYYY!!!" Nicoletta screamed with deep-red, unfocused eyes, and an immeasurably large aura surrounded her body.

Fore felt fear for the first time in his life as he watched the swaying and drooling Nicoletta approach him. Faced with such a sight, he ran.

"Come on, are you not going to attack me? I guess you won't give me the ultimate pain unless I attack you first. Oh yeah, if I do that, then I'll be able to experience the blissful agony of a counter!"

"D-d-don't underestimate me, you lowly vampire!" Fore bellowed as if to distract himself from his own quaking and charged at Nicoletta. He then performed the strongest martial arts technique he knew, called "You Belong to Me and Only Me," and chanted a spell called *Pachizoma* to send magic power inside her body and burn it.

...However, Nicoletta didn't even flinch.

"Mwa-ha-ha-ha-ha-ha!! Yes, that's what I want. But that was just a tickle. That wasn't strong enough for my body to register as pain. Show me more of your real strength! You Six Sages are the strongest and most terrible the human world has to offer, right? Give me the finest pain you can muster!"

"Wha...? You asked for it...!"

Fore used self-strengthening magic to increase his attack power as high as possible and unleashed his most ultimate of secret techniques. However, not only did Nicoletta not seem to feel any of it, but his attacks also seemed to please her.

Flummoxed and shaken at this paradoxical opponent, Fore trembled.

At the same time, Wonn kicked Mako with a killing move that he embarrassingly referred to as "Super Ultimate Gale of Darkness X Silver Wings Midnight Sun," sending the demon crashing hard into the wall. The iron facade crumbled, covering Mako with a pile of rubble and dust as she hit the floor.

"Phew. That was quite fun. It's been a long time since I've faced someone this strong," said Wonn, breathing heavily. His body was shaking from exhaustion, but he was confident Mako was defeated, so he made no effort to hide it.

No opponent of his had ever taken that attack and managed to stand afterward. This demon may have been the strongest member of the Demon Army's Four Demon Generals, but there was no way she would be able to move.

"If not for the power I've absorbed from the Demon Lord, I may have actually lost. You were a worthy enemy. I'm just a little stronger and a little more experienced. You should take this defeat with pride when you awake in the next world."

Wonn slowly approached his bested opponent, clutching his injured and aching right shoulder.

"Well, demons tend to be hard to kill. I'll cut off her head just to be sure," he muttered. A quick spell was all it took to conjure a knife in his right hand. As the leader of the Six Sages, he was a ruthless planner and decision-maker, and he never hesitated to do what was necessary to achieve his goals. His plan would be complete once he confirmed his opponent's death.

There was no room for mercy, even against an adorable beast girl.

However...

"Huh?!"

...the mountain of rubble suddenly exploded, sending countless stones soaring toward Wonn. He batted them away in irritation and then saw something that defied reason.

"Hmm, guess I really have no choice but to use this power."

Mako, whom he should have finished off already, was standing there nonchalantly, wiping sand off herself. A golden aura was flickering around her body.

"What...? How...?!"

In the best-case scenario, she should have been breathing her final breaths. But that wasn't the strangest thing about this. All the deep wounds he had inflicted on her throughout their intense battle had vanished.

"Ah, did I surprise you? Well, I guess this would. I don't ever use this ability, and the conditions required to activate it are kind of ridiculous. Also, my injuries are healed *for now*, but you can bet I'm gonna pay for this later."

Mako's easygoing manner seemed a stark contrast from Wonn, who was breaking into a nervous sweat.

"That radiant glow... Don't tell me, is this the power spoken of in beastman legend—?"

"Oh yeah. That's right. I bear the Golden Soul. I suppose this weird tradition *does* go back over three hundred years, so it makes sense that you know about it, *meow*."

Mako licked her arm, incredibly closing up a wound.

"I'm pretty sure this ability is only given to one demon in the entire Beastman Tribe. I don't really remember. It's apparently some kind of soul containing a piece of the ancient beastman god's power. It wasn't all that interesting, so I don't know the details."

"This is impossible... The Golden Soul should only manifest to protect the chief of the Beastman Tribe. You fight to save the Demon Lord! How did you tap into the power?!"

Mako frowned in irritation.

"...That's why I said the conditions are ridiculous. Anyway, I don't know anything about this custom. I am a beastman demon, but the others of my kind are selfish and arrogant, and I couldn't care less about them. Doesn't everyone choose who they want to protect for themselves anyway? I'll take that over someone deciding my loyalties for me any day."

Wonn sensed the power flowing from Mako and gulped.

"Are you saying you chose the Demon Lord as your guardian...? A savage beastman demon like you couldn't select someone from outside your tribe—"

"Are you listening?" Mako interjected with a sigh, "Surroundings, rumors, tribes—none of that matters. Those are all just assumptions you made on your own. I don't want to be tied down by laws and traditions; that kind of stuff has nothing to do with me. Your limited viewpoint is so typical of humans."

"What...?"

Wonn could not bring himself to attack now that he was facing an opponent who wielded this fearsome power. More importantly, his body was still crying out in pain from the last fight.

"Ah, also, I chose the Demon Lord as my guardian because she gives me no special treatment. Naturally, I had plenty of other reasons.

She's nothing like you. You talk like you know everything when all your knowledge is only based on your own biases."

Wonn ground his teeth in frustration, unable to even respond.

"I'm really fortunate this activated, though, given all the conditions required. If I hadn't already known your weakness beforehand, you probably would've killed me."

"Weakness...?!"

"That's right. The Hero and Cass did some intense research on the internet. Ah, did it not occur to you that everything about you, including strategies to take you down, was easily accessible online? You really don't have a sense for modern times."

"That's imposs—"

"Oops, I said too much... Eh, it doesn't matter. Let's finish this," Mako stated, eyes blazing with power.

Wonn cursed under his breath. Hesitation would spell his doom. Quick as he could manage, the old man threw up a defensive magic shield around himself.

"Too slow."

With leg strength significantly more incredible than before, Mako closed the distance between her and Wonn instantly and punched him square in the chest. The blow far surpassed any she had thrown previously, and it penetrated the barrier handily.

"Gah!!"

Blood gushed from the old man's mouth. Still, Mako showed no mercy. Not because she had almost been killed but because the dearest person in her life had been hurt. Mercy was no longer something the demon needed to concern herself with.

"This place seems pretty sturdy. Guess I might as well make use of that," Mako mused to herself. She tossed Wonn up in the air, then kicked off a wall rapidly to attack him over fifty times a second.

"*Arrrrgh!*"

Wonn was the strongest of the Six Sages, yet he was helpless in the face of Mako's many strikes.

"You all hurt the pure and kindhearted Demon Lord!" Mako cried, raising her voice to a yell for the first time in the fight. The gold aura burned bright around her. "*You'll pay for that!!*"

The tomb echoed with the sounds of Mako's lightning-quick attacks and Wonn's pained shrieks. Thus, the strongest member of the Demon Generals had defeated the strongest member of the Six Sages.

Meanwhile, the battle between Oniko and Tew was near its own climax.

"You damn geezer!!" Oniko screamed, swinging her club forcefully at Tew C, who had been a left arm. The attack connected, splitting the little man in half. "Die already!"

She then thrust her club into the torso of Tew F, who had been a right leg. That just made Tew D laugh unsettlingly. No blood ran through the clones' bodies, and the smell of rotten flesh filled the air.

The two halves of Tew C joined back together.

"As I said, I'm immortal. No attacks of yours will damage me. You're simply wasting your energy."

Oniko cursed to herself, looking visibly frustrated. The other four Tews (A, B, D, and E) then charged at her simultaneously. She did her best to fight them off with her club, but just as Tew said, she didn't seem to injure a single one of them.

"You goddamn monster!"

"Hmph. I'd rather not hear that from an ogre like you."

Catching Oniko off guard for a second, all the Tews launched explosive magic and sent her flying. She may have been fine against one spell, but avoiding six coming from different directions was impossible.

Oniko was running out of energy, but Tew showed no sign of exhaustion and had no visible injuries. Anyone observing this one-sided battle would undoubtedly have declared victory for Tew. Oniko hung her head after she landed.

"Ha-ha… Ha-ha-ha…" However, she then began to quietly laugh.

"…What's so funny?" asked the Tew that had grown from his head, coming to an abrupt stop.

"I finally figured out your little secret."

Through the bruises and cuts, Oniko's face radiated confidence. It looked as though she'd already won.

"You're a zombie, aren't you? I'm surprised. Usually, the undead that have unfinished business in this world or impure souls are reborn as demons. You're able to maintain yourself and your humanity as you split off and reproduce your body. I'll bet you absorbed many souls while performing zombie research, overwrote their wills with your own memories, preserved your body in culture fluid in a halfway state before turning into a demon, then used some forbidden spell to create a body that doesn't die. That about right?"

If the Hero had been there, he probably would have pretended to understand what she had said by saying, *Ahh, that makes total sense.*

"Hmph, what does it matter that you figured that out? By solving my secret, you've only proved I am invincible. Furthermore, thanks to the power I took from the Demon Lord, this body will never know injury, and it will never feel fatigued. That's how incredibly strong your master was. With this strength, I feel ready to resume my research on eternal youth."

Oniko looked at Tew incredulously and laughed again.

"Tell me one thing, old man. Can you really say that you're 'living'?"

"...Huh?"

"Whether human or demon, eternal life does not guarantee happiness. Our lives shine bright because of our limited time. This world would rot if it were full of idiots like you sages with your old-fashioned way of thinking," Oniko declared, angrily slamming her club into the ground. "Life is something you are entrusted with. We teach our children about its preciousness. That's why we do our best during our limited time to live and grow, which is how we make progress as a society. Just look at the Demon Lord. After many long years of conflict between demons and humans, it was her generation that finally realized the futility of our discord."

Tew clicked his tongue in irritation, and Oniko continued.

"The current era does not need old legends like you who think nothing of life. I don't like humans too much myself, but I know there are good people among them. You sages are sacrificing lives for stupid self-satisfaction. That won't get you anywhere. None of you will find happiness. Understand?"

Oniko reached out an arm and opened her palm.

"It's about time you old geezers kicked the bucket."

Tew ground his teeth in frustration, his calm expression finally waning.

"...You talk a big game, daughter of the ogres. But that is not going to help you. Without a way to properly combat me, my victory cannot be overturned."

"You sure I don't have a way to beat you?" Oniko inquired with a mischievous smile.

"…What?"

"I said it earlier. You're a zombie. That means you're weak to revival magic that purifies souls and sends them to the next life."

Tew burst out laughing.

"Revival magic? Ha, you may be right. But that only works against souls in coffins. No such spell could penetrate my body. I also highly doubt a demon could use light-elemental magic, though I welcome the effort."

"…In what era did you hear that demons can't use light-elemental magic? Hate to break it to you, but you're mistaken. We demons learn and progress. The idea that we can't use light-elemental magic is just another arrogant misconception of yours."

A ball of holy light appeared in front of Oniko's right hand. There was no mistaking its divine energy.

"What the…?!"

"By the way, my light-elemental magic is still low-level. However, the Demon Lord can use all the advanced resurrection spells that humans can. That is what we call *progress*."

"…Huh. Don't get full of yourself. Even if you can use such magic, all I have to do is evade it."

"…I'd like to see you dodge this," Oniko stated with a grin.

The luminous sphere hovering above her right hand split into five.

"It's a good thing I received magic power from the Demon Lord the other day. Thanks to that, I was able to learn advanced revival spells that are guaranteed to destroy you."

All the Tews paled.

"No, you couldn't have—"

He recalled all the times that Oniko had pierced him with her club and split him in two. If, by chance, she had planted *that* revival spell inside his bodies at the same time…

"That expression tells me you already understand what's happening. Then let's get this over with. As soon as I give the command, my magic will automatically activate within all six of your bodies."

The resurrection spell she used brought party members back to life automatically when they died, making it extremely convenient to cast before entering a difficult battle.

Immediately, Tew comprehended that this situation could not be worse for him. "N-no, don't!"

All six of Tew's bodies charged at Oniko together, and she clasped her hand tightly around the five balls of light.

"*Autolife.*"

Five of Tew's bodies burst simultaneously.

"*AAAaaaAAAaaaAAAA!!!*"

The original Tew screamed in terrible pain. Not a shred of his copies remained, but because they had been formed from parts of his body and were connected to his brain, he felt the agony of all their destructions.

"What a disgusting fireworks show," Oniko remarked. She had decided not to obliterate the original, perhaps because she wanted to honor her vow to the Demon Lord not to kill even in such a dire situation. It was also possible she aimed to deny the sage release from his pain.

"*AAAaaaAAA, AaAa, AAAaaaAAA!!!*"

Tew's screams no longer sounded human. His entire body began to emit an indescribable noise, and his arms, legs, and torso crumbled. One could say he was finally being punished for all the lives he had sacrificed in pursuit of his foolish goals.

"Well, you are a zombie. You can live just fine as a head."

Oniko had won. Even if Tew attacked her again, he wouldn't be able to accomplish much without a body. Still, Oniko wasn't foolish. Her opponent was one of the famed Six Sages. She wasn't going anywhere until what remained of Tew was unconscious.

"Mwa-ha-ha-ha-ha! Have you finally run out of magic power, fallen angel?"

A dull *whack* sounded in the tomb as Thrie kicked Pino in the side and sent her flying into a wall. The blow snapped multiple ribs. Blood bubbled up from Pino's mouth. Her defense-boosting spell had ended.

"…"

Yet Pino still had life in her eyes. Then, as if enjoying herself, she looked up at Thrie and laughed.

"Huh? Did I say something funny?"

Thrie was a total airhead, and he couldn't understand why Pino was laughing from her clearly inferior position. To him, it seemed his triumph was a foregone conclusion.

"It took a while, but my preparation is complete," Pino declared weakly, and she flapped her black wings to fly up near the ceiling of the chamber. A dark aura was drifting from her battered form.

"Preparation? Ha-ha, what are you talking about?" Thrie responded, dismissing his opponent's words with a laugh.

"Foolish question. Preparation for defeating you."

"Defeating me? Hoh-hoh-hoh! You've been on the defensive the entire time, and now you're saying you can best me? That's rich. You know that your magic has done nothing more than scratch me, right? Quit your bluffing and surrender already."

Thrie spoke with utmost assurance, but he did have a point—Pino had struck him with hundreds of advanced spells, but they hadn't even slowed the sage down. It was a testament to how insurmountable Thrie's physical strength was. Without something truly miraculous, it seemed Pino was doomed.

"...You're probably right that I can't defeat you with magic alone. Or should I say, *with my magic alone.*"

"Huh?"

Thrie had absolutely no idea what Pino was getting at, but then he suddenly caught sight of purple magic circles that dotted the walls of the tomb.

"What in the...?" Thrie could not hide his shock. Growing panicked, he looked this way and that.

"You did a wonderful job of chasing me throughout the entire tomb, Thrie. And as you did, you were unknowingly leaking the Demon Lord's magic power and feeding my magic circles."

"The Demon Lord's magic power...! Y-you can't mean...?!"

"That's right. This is my homage to the forbidden Magic Pentagram that you all used to restrain the Demon Lord. Imitation is the sincerest form of flattery, but I don't respect you at all, so I suppose it would be more accurate to say I stole the array to give you a taste of irony." Pino spoke very matter-of-factly, but there was a pep to her voice as if she was finally getting a chance to vent her anger.

"Did you not wonder why I was doing nothing but soaring around the tomb and evading your attacks? I thank you for behaving as I anticipated."

Thrie could be thickheaded at times, but that didn't mean he was stupid. Hundreds of magic circles surrounded him, and he knew full well how much trouble he was in.

"I—I, uh... Well, you're a gross demon loser!"

Sadly, all he was able to do was respond with an insult that demonstrated his miserably limited vocabulary.

"All I hear are the cries of a man who realizes he's lost. Still, if I hadn't known beforehand that you specialized in physical combat, I probably wouldn't have been able to pull off this strategy... Guess I have *him* to thank for that..."

Pino then raised her hands like a conductor at an orchestral performance.

"All right, I think I've given you enough explanation. One last thing, though. The power these magic circles sapped from you belongs to the Demon Lord... However, seeing as it's been tainted with your filth, I can't return it to her."

Thrie assumed a stance, summoned up the last of his strength, and took position to charge at Pino.

"Prepare to be purged with the power of my magic circles," the fallen angel declared.

"Don't get cocky! You're just a failed, sullied creature from the heavens!!!" Thrie screamed.

He leaped at Pino, but her attacks proved too swift for him. Hundreds of powerful blasts erupted from the magic circles, ripping through him.

"Argh, gah, hyeee, oough!"

Thrie screamed pathetically as a hundred, a thousand, ten thousand surges of energy buffeted him without pause.

The magic the Six Sages had leeched from the Demon Lord was supreme, and this demonstration of Pino's made it abundantly clear why magic circles were considered taboo throughout the world. These arrays strengthened the power they absorbed before launching it, making them function as a kind of never-ending firing squad.

And Thrie was the unlucky one caught in the middle of them all. Even if he was one of the Six Sages and possessed brawn greater than any other human in the world, there was nothing that could withstand such an onslaught.

"Here's a piece of advice," Pino began, watching her victim without a hint of pity. "You called me both an *angel* and a *fallen angel*, but I am neither." She narrowed her eyes. "I am a loyal servant of the Demon Lord, a *demon* who was given a second chance. Don't get that wrong again."

Thrie had already lost consciousness from the uncountable number of beams tearing through him, the sound of which filled the tomb with a harmony reminiscent of classical music.

"Not that you can hear me right now anyway." Pino turned and dismissed the magic circles with a snap.

Even if Thrie managed to attack her again, he'd been weakened to the point where the Hero would've been a challenge for him. Pino confirmed that her opponent's connection to the Magic Pentagram barrier had been severed and headed outside to save the Demon Lord.

NANNY
Once her magic power is fully absorbed, I'll transfer my soul into her empty shell
01:30

NANNY
I'll have the body of a 17-year-old again
01:30

HERO
...I'm not sure I want to ask, but what are you going to do after you get her body?
Read 01:31

NANNY
Fufufufufu
01:31

NANNY
I'll build the reverse harem of my dreams!!!
01:31

HERO
Uhhhh...
Read 01:31

NANNY
All the men in the world, including the other sages, will become my servants!!
01:31

HERO
Yeah, but
Read 01:31

HERO
you'll still be a rotten old woman on the inside. You won't stand a chance in hell of creating that reverse harem, no matter how attractive you are
Read 01:32

NANNY
Why you little...
01:32

HERO
You've already lived for over 300 years by swapping bodies and doing who knows what else
Read 01:32

HERO
It's time for you to go, you disgusting, ugly old bird!
Read 01:32

NANNY
I'LL KILL YOU!!!!!
01:33

☆MAKO☆
Pino, update?
03:02

♪PINO♪
Sure
03:03

♪PINO♪
I arrived just as Hamige, Sunege, and the sage all knocked one another out
03:03

♪PINO♪
The brothers are both unconscious and seriously ill. I'll head over once I finish healing them
03:03

ONIKO
That's kind of you
03:03

NICOLETTA
When are you and Hamige gonna make it official?
03:03

♪PINO♪
I hate you
03:04

♪PINO♪
How are things by you?
03:04

☆MAKO☆
I don't know. We haven't entered the tower yet
03:04

♪PINO♪
? What are you doing?
03:04

☆MAKO☆
We gave Nicoletta a beating
03:04

ONIKO
She was still way too excited after beating her sage, so we had to knock some sense into her
03:04

NICOLETTA
Can't stop. Won't stop...
03:05

♪PINO♪
Should stop
03:05

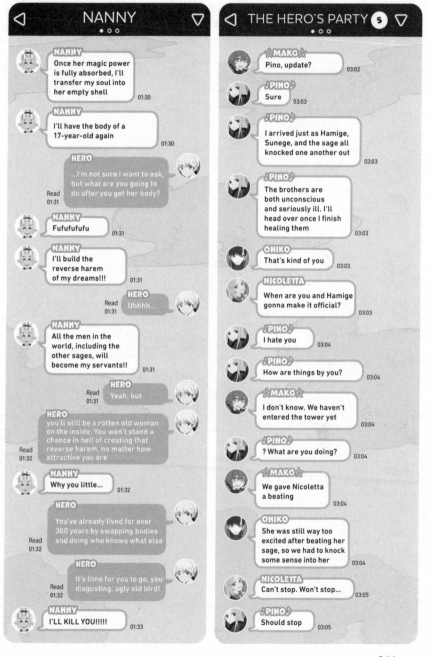

♪PINO♪
The brothers are both still out cold, but I'm done healing them 03:32

♪PINO♪
I'm gonna head to the top floor 03:32

☆MAKO☆
Rogerrr 03:33

♪PINO♪
What's happening up there? 03:33

☆MAKO☆
Uhhh
The Hero is fighting Nanny 03:33

♪PINO♪
Gotcha. Sorry
Didn't mean to interrupt in the middle of a battle 03:33

ONIKO
No, we're actually hiding behind a pillar 03:33

♪PINO♪
...Huh? 03:34

NICOLETTA
Mako stopped us 03:34

NICOLETTA
She's afraid we'll screw things up if we interfere 03:34

♪PINO♪
What in the world does that mean?! The Demon Lord is our first priority, Mako!!! 03:34

♪PINO♪
We also can't let Nanny get away with betraying us!! 03:34

☆MAKO☆
That's true, but... 03:34

☆MAKO☆
The plan to save the Demon Lord has been going really well
and that's mostly thanks to the Hero. We should trust him 03:36

♪PINO♪
He hasn't done anything!
He just came up with the plan! 03:36

♪PINO♪
And... Right, Cass! Her information is what enabled us to defeat the sages!! 03:37

☆MAKO☆
Sure, probably 03:37

☆MAKO☆
but we couldn't have made it this far without him 03:37

☆MAKO☆
We would've rushed to our deaths 03:37

♪PINO♪
Rrrrgh... 03:37

♪PINO♪
Nicoletta! Oniko!
Are you two okay with this?! 03:37

NICOLETTA
Calm down, Pino 03:38

NICOLETTA
If the Hero loses, we'll just defeat Nanny ourselves
That's all 03:38

ONIKO
I, for one, want to see the fruits of the Hero's training 03:38

☆MAKO☆
Why are you getting so worked up anyway, Pino? 03:38

♪PINO♪
I just want to save our master as soon as possible!!
03:40

☆MAKO☆
Again...
03:40

☆MAKO☆
I really think leaving this to the Hero will work out. Give him a chance
03:40

♪PINO♪
NOOO!!!!!
Even if he does manage to save the Demon Lord, this will just deepen her fixation on him!
03:41

NICOLETTA
...What's wrong with that?
03:41

ONIKO
I didn't like the Hero much at first, either
03:41

ONIKO
But he doesn't seem like a bad guy to me
and I think the Demon Lord needs him in her life
03:42

♪PINO♪
What?!
03:42

ONIKO
She's always looked so gloomy
03:42

ONIKO
but
03:42

ONIKO
since meeting the Hero, she's been so happy
03:42

♪PINO♪
Don't be ridiculous...!
03:43

☆MAKO☆
Come on, Pino, you know better than that
03:45

♪PINO♪
What do you mean?!
03:45

☆MAKO☆
You know he's a good guy
03:45

♪PINO♪
Wh-what are you...?
03:46

♪PINO♪
Don't put words in my mouth!!
It's not like I think he's kind at heart!!
Or that we can entrust the Demon Lord to him!!!
03:46

♪PINO♪
I would never think that kind of thing...
03:46

♪PINO♪
Never ever!!!
03:46

NICOLETTA
There she goes
03:46

☆MAKO☆
So annoying, meow (-_-;)
03:47

♪PINO♪
Shut up!!!
03:47

♪PINO♪
Enough about that!!!
How's the Hero's battle going?!
03:47

ONIKO
Hmm
Surprisingly well. It looks like Nanny has lost some strength
03:47

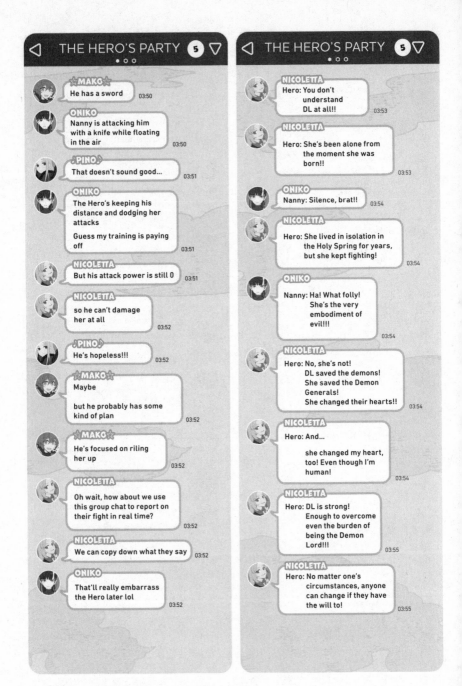

☆MAKO☆
He has a sword 03:50

ONIKO
Nanny is attacking him with a knife while floating in the air 03:50

♪PINO♪
That doesn't sound good... 03:51

ONIKO
The Hero's keeping his distance and dodging her attacks
Guess my training is paying off 03:51

NICOLETTA
But his attack power is still 0 03:51

NICOLETTA
so he can't damage her at all 03:52

♪PINO♪
He's hopeless!!! 03:52

☆MAKO☆
Maybe
but he probably has some kind of plan 03:52

☆MAKO☆
He's focused on riling her up 03:52

NICOLETTA
Oh wait, how about we use this group chat to report on their fight in real time? 03:52

NICOLETTA
We can copy down what they say 03:52

ONIKO
That'll really embarrass the Hero later lol 03:52

NICOLETTA
Hero: You don't understand DL at all!! 03:53

NICOLETTA
Hero: She's been alone from the moment she was born!! 03:53

ONIKO
Nanny: Silence, brat!! 03:54

NICOLETTA
Hero: She lived in isolation in the Holy Spring for years, but she kept fighting! 03:54

ONIKO
Nanny: Ha! What folly! She's the very embodiment of evil!!! 03:54

NICOLETTA
Hero: No, she's not! DL saved the demons! She saved the Demon Generals! She changed their hearts!! 03:54

NICOLETTA
Hero: And...
she changed my heart, too! Even though I'm human! 03:54

NICOLETTA
Hero: DL is strong! Enough to overcome even the burden of being the Demon Lord!!! 03:55

NICOLETTA
Hero: No matter one's circumstances, anyone can change if they have the will to! 03:55

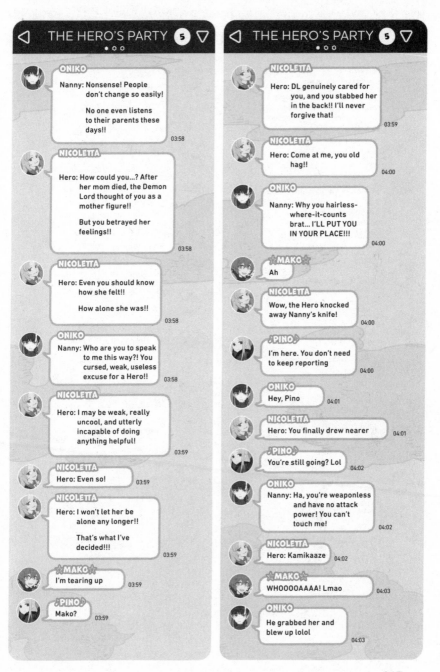

ONIKO

Nanny: Nonsense! People don't change so easily!

No one even listens to their parents these days!!

03:58

NICOLETTA

Hero: How could you...? After her mom died, the Demon Lord thought of you as a mother figure!!

But you betrayed her feelings!!

03:58

NICOLETTA

Hero: Even you should know how she felt!!

How alone she was!!

03:58

ONIKO

Nanny: Who are you to speak this way?! You cursed, weak, useless excuse for a Hero!!

03:58

NICOLETTA

Hero: I may be weak, really uncool, and utterly incapable of doing anything helpful!

03:59

NICOLETTA

Hero: Even so!

03:59

NICOLETTA

Hero: I won't let her be alone any longer!!

That's what I've decided!!!

03:59

☆MAKO☆

I'm tearing up

03:59

♪PINO♪

Mako?

03:59

NICOLETTA

Hero: DL genuinely cared for you, and you stabbed her in the back!! I'll never forgive that!

03:59

NICOLETTA

Hero: Come at me, you old hag!!

04:00

ONIKO

Nanny: Why you hairless-where-it-counts brat... I'LL PUT YOU IN YOUR PLACE!!!

04:00

☆MAKO☆

Ah

NICOLETTA

Wow, the Hero knocked away Nanny's knife!

04:00

♪PINO♪

I'm here. You don't need to keep reporting

04:00

ONIKO

Hey, Pino

04:01

NICOLETTA

Hero: You finally drew nearer

04:01

♪PINO♪

You're still going? Lol

04:02

ONIKO

Nanny: Ha, you're weaponless and have no attack power! You can't touch me!

04:02

NICOLETTA

Hero: Kamikaaze

04:02

☆MAKO☆

WHOOOOAAAA! Lmao

04:03

ONIKO

He grabbed her and blew up lolol

04:03

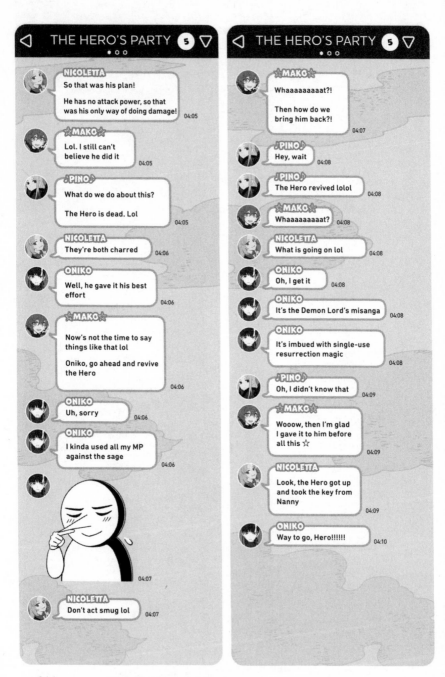

NICOLETTA
So that was his plan!

He has no attack power, so that was his only way of doing damage!
04:05

☆MAKO☆
Lol. I still can't believe he did it
04:05

♪PINO♪
What do we do about this?

The Hero is dead. Lol
04:05

NICOLETTA
They're both charred
04:06

ONIKO
Well, he gave it his best effort
04:06

☆MAKO☆
Now's not the time to say things like that lol

Oniko, go ahead and revive the Hero
04:06

ONIKO
Uh, sorry
04:06

ONIKO
I kinda used all my MP against the sage
04:06

04:07

NICOLETTA
Don't act smug lol
04:07

☆MAKO☆
Whaaaaaaaaat?!

Then how do we bring him back?!
04:07

♪PINO♪
Hey, wait
04:08

♪PINO♪
The Hero revived lolol
04:08

☆MAKO☆
Whaaaaaaaaat?
04:08

NICOLETTA
What is going on lol
04:08

ONIKO
Oh, I get it
04:08

ONIKO
It's the Demon Lord's misanga
04:08

ONIKO
It's imbued with single-use resurrection magic
04:08

♪PINO♪
Oh, I didn't know that
04:09

☆MAKO☆
Wooow, then I'm glad I gave it to him before all this ☆
04:09

NICOLETTA
Look, the Hero got up and took the key from Nanny
04:09

ONIKO
Way to go, Hero!!!!!!
04:10

ZA
(SILENCE)

DEMON LORD

DEMON LORD
Um
04:20

HERO
Uh
Read 04:20

HERO
Hey
Read 04:21

DEMON LORD
Hero
04:21

HERO
Huh?
Read 04:21

DEMON LORD
thdk
04:21

DEMON LORD
Thank you
04:21

DEMON LORD
for saving me...
04:21

HERO
S
Read 04:22

HERO
Sure...
Read 04:22

DEMON LORD
...
04:22

HERO
...
Read 04:22

DEMON LORD
...
04:22

HERO
...
Read 04:22

HERO Read 04:23 So, DL

DEMON LORD Um, Hero 04:23

HERO Read 04:23 Huh?!

DEMON LORD Wha?! 04:23

HERO Read 04:23 Oh, I'm sorry!!

DEMON LORD Sorry about that!! 04:23

HERO Read 04:24 DL!!

DEMON LORD Hero!! 04:24

HERO Read 04:24 Ah!

DEMON LORD Ah! 04:24

DEMON LORD ...Haha 04:24

HERO Read 04:24 Ahaha

HERO Read 04:24 What're we doing?

DEMON LORD Good question lol 04:25

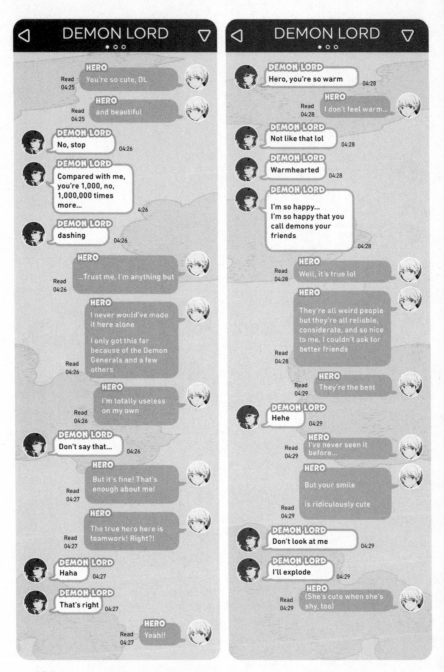

IF THE RPG WORLD HAD SOCIAL MEDIA...

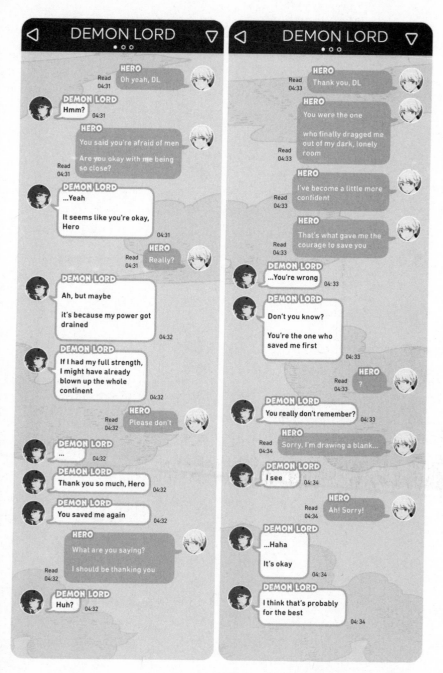

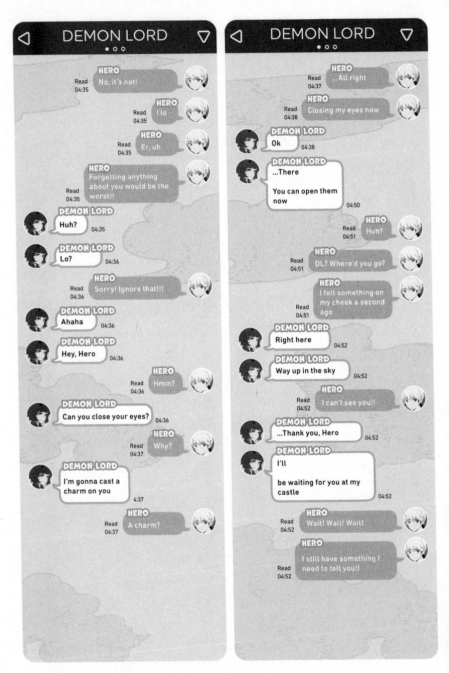

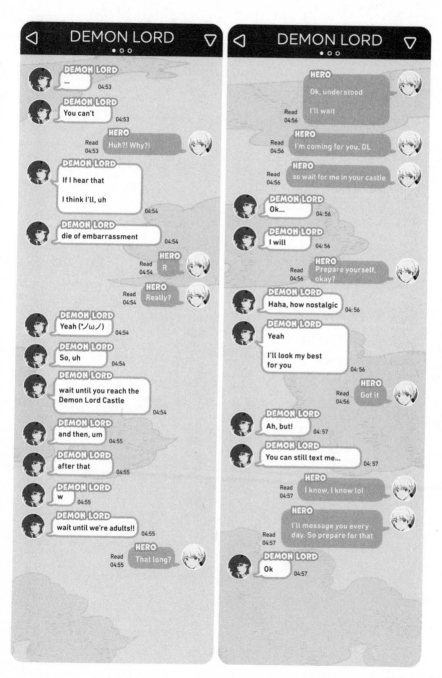

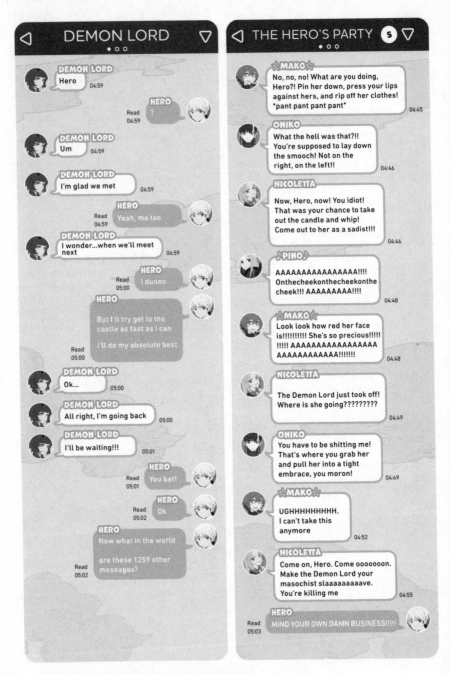

IF THE RPG WORLD HAD SOCIAL MEDIA...

Thus, the Six Sages' plot entitled "Demon Lord Magic Power Rescue Operation / Six Sages Revival Ceremony / Parental Guidance Advised" was thwarted by the Hero and his comrades. The Demon Lord was rescued, and she happily took to the skies and soared back to her home.

Success wouldn't have been possible without cooperation from the princes of Tomorrow Castle in Beginnerland and the rare uniting of humans and demons against a common foe.

Thanks to the power of the internet, the news that a revival attempt of the Six Sages was thwarted spread like wildfire. False information and rumors abounded, of course, and counterefforts to divide humans and demons sprang up. Only the gods knew the truth of what happened that day.

Yet for the direct participants, there was no doubt that the incident brought people together and helped form a deeper bond between divided societies.

"Ugh…"

Hamige, who had been knocked unconscious at the end of his battle with Fyve, stirred in the dark tomb located to the east of Balse.

"I'm…alive," he said hoarsely and touched the tough armor he had equipped. It was riddled with holes, but there wasn't a single injury on him.

He had somehow managed to dodge all of Fyve's signature instant-death spells, but the physical-piercing spell Fyve spent the last of his strength to use should have ran him through. Hamige recalled meeting the attack with a finishing move of his own, one that used his Divine Sword Eidrian. Everything past that was a murky unknown.

"Ah, Lady Pino…and Sunege!"

Hamige sprang up, paying no heed to his aching body. Quickly, he searched for his younger brother, who'd stood with him against the villainous sage. It turned out there was no need for concern—Sunege was lying right behind him. The younger prince was sleeping soundly, and to Hamige's relief, he was also miraculously unhurt.

"Thank goodness. We're both alive."

After a sigh of relief, Hamige spotted a black feather on the ground.

"This is…"

He quickly picked it up, looking the thing over intently. Growing a little overexcited, Hamige decided that this meant his beloved Pino must have rushed to them out of great concern. She had rescued Hamige and his brother from the brink of death.

"She hurried all the way here for my sake? Oh, Lady Pino… You're so brave and beautiful…"

Like someone hit on the head too many times or a fool who

couldn't take a hint, Hamige decided to take this feather as a sign of Pino's love.

"Wahhh!"

Sunege suddenly jumped to his feet, shivering at his elder sibling's creepy words. Hamige was truly in a class of his own.

"Hey, Sunege. You're awake. It looks like Lady Pino graced you with her healing as well," said Hamige.

"Urgh… My whole body still hurts a little. But it looks like we managed somehow, bro," Sunege replied.

The pair looked each other in the eye for a few seconds, then burst out laughing at how ragged the other looked. They embraced, happy to be alive.

Any jealousy or ill will fostered by a difference in ability between the duo vanished. They'd risked themselves together and, most importantly, had found something worth fighting for.

"…You two are loud as ever."

Hamige and Sunege looked up to see that someone was watching them as they laughed.

It was Pino, a member of the Demon Generals—officer of the Demon Army and fallen angel prone to sudden mood swings. After confirming that the Demon Lord had returned to the castle, she had come to check on Hamige and Sunege and thank them for their cooperation.

Truthfully, she only did so after being pushed by Oniko, who'd insisted, *"He said he'd do anything for you; now show some manners and go talk to them!"*

"L-L-L-Lady Pino!!" Hamige pushed aside the brother he had just embraced and ran toward Pino. Her face spasmed.

"Hwuh! Don't come near me, you creep! And don't toss your brother aside like that!"

"A-ah, sorry, Sunege! But wow, you really are a kindhearted demon who places value on siblings and family. My love for you burns ever brighter!"

"Shut up."

"H-hey, Bro, don't forget about me! I'm injured!"

Laughter filled the tomb, possibly due to a release of tension from having survived what undoubtedly had felt like certain doom. When things quieted down, Pino spoke up.

"...I've said as much already, but we couldn't have rescued the Demon Lord without your help. I'm grateful for that."

"There is no need for thanks. These criminals broke human law. As a prince of Tomorrow Castle, it is my duty to make them pay for their crimes," responded Hamige.

"Yeah. Don't worry about it, Pino. We should be the ones apologizing. We've had the Demon Army and the Demon Generals all wrong. You're the best friends I've ever had, yo!" appended Sunege.

After hearing such kind words from humans who had once treated her with hostility, Pino softened her cold expression for the first time since entering the room.

"Talking with you two makes my head hurt. Anyway, to wrap things up, the Six Sages are all still alive. They don't deserve an ounce of sympathy, but we decided they're not even worth killing. The Demon Lord has also forbidden her direct subordinates from taking lives. That said, this is a human problem. I trust I can leave them to you?"

"Of course. We will apprehend these criminals. They've committed a first-degree violation of magic law. The king and the citizens of

Balse were likely all under their control. My country will provide support on that front as well," declared Hamige.

"That's a big help."

"It's all good, girl! This incident was borne of human greed, so we need to be the ones to put an end to it!" exclaimed Sunege.

Pino smiled again, then spread her black wings and turned toward the entrance.

"Ah, wait, Lady Pino!" Hamige called.

"...What is it?" Pino inquired without turning around.

"You... After defeating your sage, you should have wanted to rush to the Demon Lord as quickly as possible. Why did you come to us first?"

After a pause, Pino answered, "I—I was just worried that you might have lost." She flapped her black wings faster to cope with the embarrassment. "D-don't get the wrong idea! It's not like I thought that coming here to heal your injuries was the least I could do to thank you for your help... I wasn't thinking anything like that at all, okay?!"

Hurriedly, she flew out of the tomb.

"Ha-ha-ha... Those Demon Generals are good people once you get to know them. That probably goes for all demons," Sunege remarked, watching Pino go with a smile.

Hamige was visibly shaking.

"My..."

"Huh? What is it, Bro?"

"*My heart...!*"

"You should keep that kinda thing to yourself, my dude," Sunege chided, exasperated. The siblings set to work arresting the remaining sages.

HERO
Allllll right

That's done
Read
11:15

☆**MAKO**☆
Yep
11:15

♪**PINO**♪
I got a text from Hamige
11:16

♪**PINO**♪
They arrested all the unconscious Six Sages

He says that because they used forbidden magic, Beginnerland's military police are going to take responsibility and deliver punishment
11:16

HERO
Wow. But will that work out?

Seems like the Six Sages are strong enough to break out of any prison
Read
11:16

♪**PINO**♪
It'll be fine
11:16

♪**PINO**♪
The Magic Pentagram is a heretical spell used to resurrect the dead

Its failure incurs consequences on the casters. They're not going to cause any trouble
11:16

HERO
Read   Consequences?
11:16

NICOLETTA
Ooh!   11:17

HERO
Read   Answer me lol
11:17

☆**MAKO**☆
How to explain...

They've become a shell of themselves. No strength, knowledge, or memories
11:18

HERO
Oh, so they're just
Read   regular old people now
11:18

♪**PINO**♪
They tried to absorb the Demon Lord's magic power

Failing at that takes a heavy toll
11:18

ONIKO
Eh, who cares? They were dead to begin with, so being alive at all is a clear win
11:19

HERO
Read   This doesn't sit right
11:19

HERO
They might've saved the world 300 years ago, but I'd like for them to use the rest of their existences to atone for their crimes
Read
11:19

NICOLETTA
Btw, Hero   11:19

Hero: DL is strong! Enough to overcome even the burden of being the Demon Lord!!
Read
03:55

NICOLETTA
Hero: No matter one's circumstances, anyone can change if they have the will lol
Read
03:55

ONIKO
Nanny: Nonsense! People don't change so easily!
11:20

NICOLETTA
Whaddaya think of this?   11:20

HERO
Ughhhh!!!!
Read   ...Can we forget this ever
11:20   happened?

HERO
Read 11:22
Please stop

HERO
Read 11:22
I'm begging you

Hero: I may be weak, really uncool, and utterly incapable of doing anything helpful!
Read 03:59

NICOLETTA
Read 03:59
Hero: Even so!

NICOLETTA
Hero: I won't let her be alone any longer!!
11:23

HERO
Read 11:23
STOPPPPPPP!

☆MAKO☆
Hey, what's the problem? I thought that was really cool lol
11:23

♪PINO♪
Well
11:24

♪PINO♪
it was also really, really corny!!!!
11:24

ONIKO
I had to really fight laughing when I was typing
11:24

HERO
Read 11:24
Damn... I thought there was no one there!

☆MAKO☆
Now you know lol
11:24

NICOLETTA
Also, Hero
11:24

HERO
Read 11:25
Huh?

NICOLETTA
...Respond to her before she stabs you
11:25

HERO
Read 11:25
...
She's sent me 898 texts. I'm scared to open them

CASS
Hey, Big Bro, I heard from Sis. Is your battle over? Sooooooo oooooooooooooooooooooooooooo oooooooooooooooooooooooooooo oooooooooooooooooooooooooooo oooooooooooooooooooooooooooo oooooooooooooooooooooooooooo oooooooooooooooooooooooooooo oooooooooooooooooooooooooooo oooooooooooooooooooooooooooo oooooooooooooooooooooooooooo oooooooooooooooooooooooooooo oooooooooooooooooooooooooooo oooooooooooooooooooooooooooo oooooooooooooooooooooooooooo oooooooooooooooooooooooooooo oooooooooooooooooooooooooooo oooooooooooooooooooooooooooo oooooooooooooooooooooo you know what you promised right? You said in exchange for my help you'd listen to anything I say, but you're taking so long to respond to me, Big Bro, your heart, your body, your brain, your blood, your everything belongs to me, so you have to respond to me, you know? Ah, I know what's going on, it's Ayase isn't it? I can smell it, you used to message me all the time, Big Bro, but you've been so cold to me lately She doesn't understand a single thing about you!!! I know you better than anyone in the whole world!!!! You have to message me, Big Bro, you belong to me, so you have to do it, come ooooooooon, Big Bro, respond to me, I want to suck your blood, Big Bro, I'm watching you, Big Bro, don't forget that I'll alllllllllways be watching you, so if you cheat or anything like that I'll slice up your body, I'll wash it, then I'll bite into your carotid artery and suuuuuuuuck all the blood that comes out without letting a single drop escape, I'll suck your body till it's completely dry

▶

PRINCESS
Demon Lord???!!! 18:20

PRINCESS
Where are you??!!!! 18:21

PRINCESS
Nanny isn't in the castle, either... 18:21

PRINCESS
📞
Missed call 18:50

PRINCESS
I don't...!
I don't know what to do without you, Demon Lord! 19:15

PRINCESS
Oh, Demon Lord...!
My one and only Demon Lord...!! 19:16

PRINCESS
Tell me how much you love me... 19:56

PRINCESS
Demon Lord: I wuv you 19:57

PRINCESS
Me: I wuv you, too... 19:57

DEMON LORD
...S-sorry, Princess
I just got back
Read 19:58

PRINCESS
HUWAAAAAAAAAAAAA AAAAAAAAAAAA!!! (sudden loss of vocabulary) 19:58

PRINCESS
Wherever did you go off to, Demon Lord? 20:18

PRINCESS
How could you leave your fiancée alone like that?! 20:18

DEMON LORD
Uhh, it's kinda hard to explain...
Read 20:19

DEMON LORD
Sorry for making you worry m(_ _)m
Read 20:19

PRINCESS
Well, I can't expect perfection. I forgive you 20:19

PRINCESS
You can make up for it by sleeping with me from now on!! 20:19

DEMON LORD
Uh, I'd rather not...
Read 20:19

20:19

DEMON LORD
By the way, did anything happen at the castle while I was away?
Read 20:20

PRINCESS
Huh? Let me think... 20:20

PRINCESS
There was someone here calling themselves a member of the "Down Below Demon Generals" 20:20

DEMON LORD
Down Below?
Read 20:20

☆MAKO☆
What the...?
I just felt a chill
20:52

♪PINO♪
Weird, I did, too
20:53

NICOLETTA
Chills feel so good
20:53

Read 20:53 — HERO That's just you

ONIKO
This sensation...
The Down Below Demon Generals have come to the Surface World
20:53

Read 20:54 — HERO Down Below DGs?

ONIKO
They're the Demon Overlord's servants
20:54

HERO
Oh, the people who DL drove into the Down Below
Read 20:54

☆MAKO☆
I haaate them
20:54

HERO Huh? Why?
Read 20:54

♪PINO♪
They are belligerent toward humans and possess unrivaled strength in combat
They will stop at nothing to achieve their goals
20:55

☆MAKO☆
Also
20:55

☆MAKO☆
the leader's a super perv
20:55

HERO Why...? Just why...?
Read 20:55

MAKAO
Helloooooo, my darling Demon Lord ♥♥ Long time no see!!!!
20:30

MAKAO
Just how long has it been?! Too long for me......teehee
20:31

MAKAO
I heard about what happened ♪ To think Nanny was a human who was planning to betray us all along!
20:31

MAKAO
The Demon Overlord sent us to this world because he's soooo worried about you, darling. He can't bear the thought of you getting hurt again ★★
20:31

MAKAO
So that means ♥ from today on, I, Makao of the Down Below Demon Generals, will be serving as your secretary!!!
20:31

20:31

DEMON LORD
...But
I have a fear of men
Read 20:32

MAKAO
Don't worry, darling
20:32

MAKAO
I'm going to take this veeeeeeeeery seriously ♥♥♥
20:32

MAKAO
Mwahahahaha (@°▽°@)!!!!!!!
20:32

DEMON LORD Why...? Just why...?
Read 20:33

YUSUKE NITTA   235

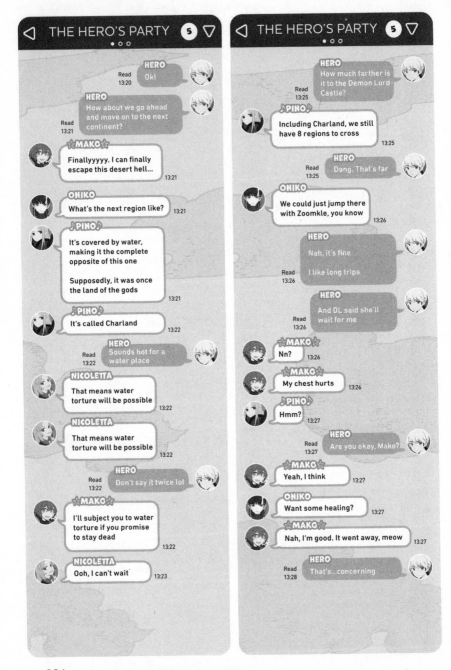

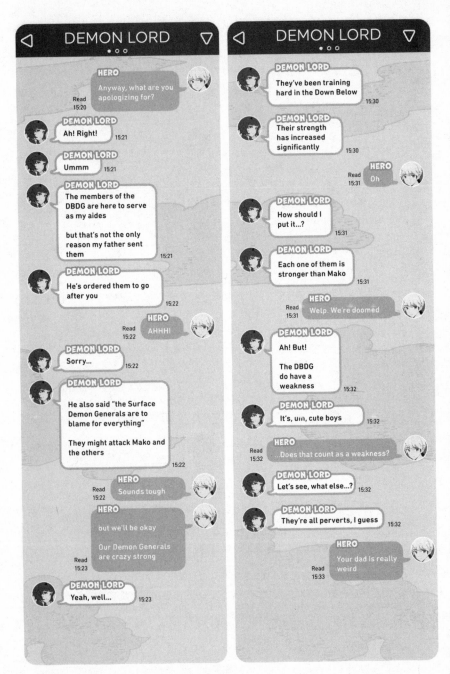

IF THE RPG WORLD HAD SOCIAL MEDIA...

Once, there existed a position at the top of society known as the Demon Lord.

The Demon Lord's breath wilted vegetation. Earth decayed beneath their feet. Clouds darkened with contaminants when they soared through the sky. Every obstacle crumbled in the face of their unyielding charge. This creature ruled over all demons as the most powerful of their kind. They were evil incarnate, surpassing the gods with might beyond human understanding.

However, that was just a rumor spread by humans—one borne out of simple prejudice and fear. In reality, the Demon Lord had a kind soul and desired to live in harmony.

The ruler had spent eight years living alone in the Holy Spring and strived to keep a promise she'd made to a young boy. She was pure, innocent, and the nicest person in the world.

"Haaah…geez."

The Demon Lord collapsed onto her bed and sighed.

She'd been feeling worried about the future ever since Makao, the member of the Down Below Demon Generals whom her father had sent to the Demon Lord Castle, arrived. Worst of all, due to her fear of men, the simple presence of one in her home had her feeling depressed.

"…Ha-ha."

Still, she smiled.

The Demon Lord wasn't alone anymore. Just recently, a few humans had worked together with demons, her bonds with her dear subordinates had deepened, and above all, she was always connected to the Hero, whom she had developed feelings for. Indeed, it was hard *not* to be happy.

The Demon Lord took out her phone and rechecked her messages. Then she looked at her chat history with the Hero, and her cheeks flushed red.

Once, there existed a position at the top of society known as the Hero.

The Hero was capable of breathing…but that was about it. His bones were wont to break from merely walking. Flying through the sky was a pipe dream to him. He couldn't manage to run for more than five seconds without needing to catch his breath. This creature was the weakest of all human beings, a shut-in with the moodiest of personalities who spent all his free time on the internet.

…However, he did have one redeeming feature: When he decided to do something or resolved to save someone, he possessed the courage to see it through.

As a hero, he was pretty inept—quite possibly the weakest person in the world. Extreme shyness kept him from talking to people, and that only scratched the surface of his inadequacies. Yet by rescuing the Demon Lord, he'd proved his own declaration.

"No matter one's circumstances, anyone can change if they have the will to!"

Those words were corny enough to make a person throw up in their mouth. Still, even as pitiful and unreliable as the Hero had been, his strong determination to save the Demon Lord *had* changed him.

He wasn't alone anymore, either. Along his journey, he'd found comrades with whom he shared mutual trust. It didn't matter that they were demons. Above all, he was always connected through social media to the Demon Lord, who'd saved him from his dark room.

[*Sigh*... Sleeping outdoors again yet again...] Once he'd sent the text, the Hero exhaled in real life as he sat in front of the bonfire at a camp his group had set up on their way to Charland.

"What did you expect, a five-star hotel?" chided Mako.

"You can burn me with a stick if you want," suggested Nicoletta.

"Shut up, masochist," spat Pino.

"Hero, the meat is done, so eat up," Oniko said.

The members of the Demon Army's Four Demon Generals all regarded him kindly.

"..."

Unfortunately, the Hero couldn't respond. They'd rescued the Demon Lord together, but it seemed his communication disorder was still going strong.

"Still silent, huh? When will he be able to talk?" wondered Oniko aloud.

"He can message us. That works just fine. No point worrying about it, *meow*," Mako answered.

"By the way, aren't you cold in that sleeping bag at night, Hero?" inquired Pino.

"Leave him be. He's probably just adopted my masochist ways by now," Nicoletta replied, speaking for the Hero.

The young man broke into a smile at their cheeriness and clumsy attempts to help him. He ignored Nicoletta's nonsense, took a haunch of meat, and sent another message in the group chat.

[Thanks, everyone.]

The members of the Demon Generals looked puzzled for a second, then they all grinned warmly.

The Demon Lord had a dream.

Her mother, who'd perished over ten years ago, was right in front of her, talking to someone in a gentle voice.

"I love you, Demon Lord."

It was the moment right before her death. The Demon Lord's younger self was there, too, wailing at her parent's side.

"I'm sure you'll have to face a lot of hardship in your life... But you'll be okay."

Her mother hugged the young Demon Lord tightly.

"I know there is someone out there who you are destined to meet. Someone who will love you, no matter if you're the Demon Lord or what kind of power you have. Don't be afraid. Take that person's hand and strive for happiness."

Tears began to flow as the Demon Lord remembered her mother's final words.

"I'm so glad I was able to bring you into this world and spend this time with you. You made me so happy. Please live. No matter what happens, rely on the people around you and keep moving forward. Do that, and you'll find happiness, just as I did in my life."

At last, the Demon Lord was able to recall the words that she'd been unable to hear over her sobbing.

"...No matter how far away I am, I will always love you, Demon Lord."

Her mother smiled affectionately. There was a brief flash of pale light, and the woman was gone.

The Demon Lord awoke with a start and realized she was crying. Feeling a little anxious, she messaged the Hero despite the late hour.

[What happened? Are you okay?] The Hero's response was quick. A deep sense of relief washed over her.

After they spent a little time texting about nothing in particular, the Demon Lord lay back down on her bed, feeling at ease.

Both the Demon Lord and the Hero would undoubtedly face many hardships from here on. Trouble would follow them for the rest of their lives.

But they would surely get through it just fine.

No matter how far apart the two of them were, they were always connected through social media, and even more importantly, in their hearts.

AFTERWORD

Thank you very much for reading *If the RPG World Had Social Media…*

I would never have thought this story that I published on the internet would get made into a book, and when I was given the offer, I was so happy that I wanted to jump for joy.

I owe the final product's existence to the project lead who reached out to me; LOL, for her beautiful character designs; and Yukinatsu Amekaze, for depicting the lovely characters in her illustrations. More than anything, however, I owe it to all of you who read and supported the original work. I'd also like to use this opportunity to thank my family, friends, colleagues, and everyone who supported me when times grew tough. I thank you from the bottom of my heart.

My pen name, Yusuke Nitta, is close to my real name, but I changed the *suke* character to one that means "help" or "save." I got the idea from my author friends when I started writing online.

I took the pen name as a show of gratitude to them and so I wouldn't forget my roots. I will work hard to live up to this name by creating stories that might help someone in a difficult spot.

ILLUSTRATOR: LOL

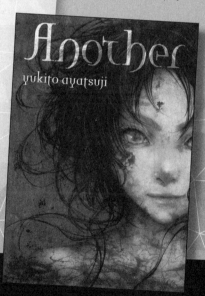